This book is dedicated to anyone that has ever dealt with a demonic entity.

"We came into this world like brother and brother,
And now let's go hand in hand, not one before another."
William Shakespeare

"But nobody can run from their own demons"
Alexander Gordon Smith

Chapter 1

The letter was buried in the pile of junk mail that covered the welcome mat, as if their apartment was trying to protect them from what was to come. If it were not for the shiny Pokémon stickers plastered across the envelope, Henk would have kicked it aside with the rest of the improvised draught excluder. He carried the manilla sleeve back into the front room.

"Hey, check this out," he said, waving the envelope in front of his brother's face.

Dave batted him away, craned his neck to watch the Japanese gameshow on the small TV. On the screen, a skinny man in a pterodactyl suit was sprinting across a wobbling bridge while several women fired cannonballs at him. "I think this guy's going to make it."

"Look," Henk said, slapping him across the back of his shaved head.

"Wait." The man on the TV took a cannonball to the face and backflipped over the edge of the rickety bridge into the abyss. "What do you want?" Dave said impatiently.

"I think it's from Maria. The one that got away."

"Well, technically, it was *us* that left, which makes *her* the one that stayed behind." Dave shot upright in his seat, "You think she wants to get the old gang back together again?"

Henk shrugged and ripped open the envelope, produced a single sheet of card that smelt of cinnamon and fresh-cut grass. "We're too old for that shit. No, this is . . ."

"What?"

"You are cordially invited to the wedding of Harman Notabaddie and Maria Wendall, blah blah blah."

"They're getting *married*?" Dave asked incredulously. In his mind, they were all still teenagers, and likely forever would be. Henk scanned the rest of the invitation, unsure how he was supposed to feel. "They're getting married," Dave muttered.

The town of Sorrow was not a place either of them would admit they thought of anymore. At fourteen, their parents had killed themselves in a bizarre yet not entirely surprising suicide pact in the mortuary. The mortician had found them stripped nude on the slabs, their clothes neatly folded in a pile beneath their heads. They'd each sawed through their throats with identical bread knives, with their mother managing to make it all the way through before she'd bled out.

It was not the first or last time a resident would take their life in a similar fashion.

Henk first noticed the underlying dread that tainted the metaphysical composition of the town when he hit puberty. He'd awoken one morning with a niggling feeling that he was forgetting something important. The room seemed smaller than it had been the night before. The air itself felt thicker. Their parents told him he was becoming a man, and he remembered thinking if that feeling of existential dread was only going to worsen, perhaps he didn't want to be a man at all.

Dave was different. Nothing phased Dave. Well, aside from their parent's death. That one stung just a little. Other than that, he'd always been like Maria—carefree and nonchalant.

As soon as Henk turned eighteen (the younger of the two) and they had full access to their inheritance, they slipped away from the Last Chance orphanage and boarded the next train out of Sorrow.

Now living in the city, not only could they afford a crappy apartment, but they'd both been able to coast by with only minimal hours put in at the local bowling alley.

Dave flicked a sandwich crust from the arm of the chair, "I hadn't thought of them for years."

Unlike Henk, who felt a mild flutter in his bowel as he pictured Maria's smile–

He stopped himself before he zoned out. It had been almost a decade. He'd never had the courage to ask her out, and now she was getting married. To the pig boy, no less. If it were anyone else, he wouldn't even consider returning to that cesspit. But it *wasn't* anyone else.

Dave stood, stretched. "You want to go?"

Henk ignored the feeling of unease that threatened to floor him as he thought of the place, tried to focus on her instead. "It would be good to see her again."

"I bet it would," Dave winked. "Might be a good chance to rack up another kill while we're there too."

Henk shook his head but smiled as he continued reading. "We're not getting involved in that craziness again. Hold on a minute, what day is it?"

"Friday?"

Henk checked his phone and saw that it was indeed Friday. "The wedding is next week. She says our accommodation is already taken care of, if we wanted to spend a few days catching up beforehand. A driver will be waiting to pick us up from the seven p.m. train, Friday the tenth. That's today, in three hours! How long has this been sitting there?!"

Dave scratched the back of his neck and turned up the TV. "Well, we're not going to make that. Let's just have a smoke."

Henk tossed the invite onto the water-stained coffee table. "Go and have a shower. We've got plenty of time before the train leaves."

"You sure you want to go back there?"

Henk wasn't sure. Truth be told, he'd not really thought past seeing Maria again. "All that was a long time ago. I'm sure."

Dave sighed as if to say, "It's your funeral," and shuffled off to the bathroom to wash away the smell of sweaty balls (he'd been on ball retrieval duty at the bowling alley earlier that day, and many of them were in desperate need of a clean).

Henk picked up the invitation again, and without realizing he was even doing it, brought it up to his nose, inhaling deeply. The aroma combined with the steady patter of the shower pulled him back to his last memories of Sorrow.

It was raining. Relentlessly.

Henk sat alone in the orphanage's conservatory, willing the roar of the water to drown his thoughts in static. It was the anniversary of his parent's death, and he couldn't help but think it was also another moment closer to his own. Why had they given their lives to the Head? Was its call that subtle, *insidious,* that they did not understand what they were doing?

Henk didn't realise that he was already under its influence, too.

It was getting harder to find anything to live for. Even their recent successes in defeating the entities that plagued the town were not enough to prevent the feelings that came when he was alone, which were worsened by Dave and Maria seeming so unperturbed by the place they called home. Whenever Henk attempted to convey his true feelings, he was met with blank stares.

Sorrow was far enough removed from the rest of society that it was generally expected the children raised in the town would get jobs in the town and start families of their own. A train passed through twice a day, once in the morning and again in the evening, and a narrow road flanked by crop fields (often flooded during heavy rains) served as the only road in and out. Add to that a general lack of phone reception and intermittent-at-best internet, and you've got all the ingredients for a self-sufficient society.

That's not to say the people of Sorrow were cut off from the outside world entirely—far from it. A postman would pass through three times a week, and the town had its own electricity and water supply. It was simply that many of the families living in Sorrow had done so for generations, and the simpler, slower pace of life was all they had ever known.

Henk knew that he was at a crossroads in his life. There was nothing left for him in Sorrow. Okay, so that wasn't *entirely* true. Maria was in Sorrow. But he already knew his dreams of running into the sunset with her would stay as that—they'd grown up together, she would never see him as anything more than a friend. He grimaced as he turned the bottle of sleeping pills over in his hand, wondering if they would numb his senses sufficiently for what he was contemplating doing. Surely it would be better than living a drawn-out existence of suffering, sprinkled with faint promises of hope.

The front door slammed. A dark figure stumbled through the ground floor, shoes squelching across the laminate. Henk winced as the overhead lights came on.

Dave shrugged his coat off and tossed it over the back of the nearest chair. "There you are. What are you doing out here in the dark, you freak?"

"Just thinking," Henk responded.

"You've been acting weird lately," Dave said, shaking himself off like a dog.

Henk slipped the pills into his pocket. He knew what he had to do, and it couldn't wait. If he stayed in this place a moment longer, he thought he'd go insane. "I need to get out of here."

"The conservatory?" Dave said, raising his voice as the rain grew increasingly violent. He gestured to the darkness beyond the window. "'Cos I know you aren't suggesting we go out there right now."

"I don't expect you to come with me, but I have to get out of town, Dave. If I don't . . . let's just say I'm starting to understand why our parents did what they did."

"Next you'll be telling me you believe all that crap about the Head poisoning people's thoughts."

"Given the shit we've been dealing with recently, is it really that far-fetched?" Henk pushed past his brother. "As I said, I don't expect you to come, but I'm going."

It wasn't until Henk produced a backpack containing several changes of clothes that Dave believed he was serious. He slid back into his sodden coat. "Give me ten minutes."

"Wait, really?"

Dave looked as indifferent as always as he said, "Sure. Why not? Hardly going to let you go alone."

Ten minutes later, they were outside Maria's parent's, wiping the rain from their eyes as if it could be causing them to hallucinate Harman's yellow Mini Cooper parked at the curb. Another local their age, Harman was homeschooled by his father and rumoured to enjoy mudwrestling with the pigs on their farm. He was known to have a short fuse and generally just be a bit of a cock.

They rushed up the cobbled path to the small overhang outside the front door, coats pulled over heads. As Henk went to knock, the door swung inward, and he almost rapped Maria square on the nose.

"Henk?" Maria looked flustered, eyes flicking between the boys on either side of her door. "Uh, what are you guys doing out there?"

Behind her, further down the hall, Harman's head could be seen peeking out from the front room. Henk was reluctant to say anything in front of him, but Harman didn't look like he was planning on leaving. "You remember what we spoke about the day we buried my parents? Well, Dave and I are leaving town. Tonight. We thought you should know, is all."

Harman stepped out into the hall. "*Leaving?*" he said, as if Henk had suggested they cut the skin off each other's faces and use them as fleshlights.

"I need to do this. Dave's coming with me—"

Maria's eyebrows shot an inch up her forehead. "Can't you sleep on it? We can talk about it in the morning once you've had a chance to think it over a little more?"

"I can't think anymore. I'm sorry. Maybe you could . . ." He couldn't bring himself to finish the sentence. Asking her to leave with them would have been hard enough without Harman there, but the guy was now practically close enough to kiss. The implication must have been easier to decipher than Henk imagined, for Maria responded without pause.

"Oh. I mean, I would, but I couldn't leave my parents, you know? My stepdad wouldn't like it."

Watching the girl he'd fantasized himself being with for several years slip through his fingers (with an audience, no less) stung more than a little. "No, of course. It wouldn't have felt right if I didn't check, though."

Harman's eyes rolled across the ceiling before settling on Maria. "Awkward."

Maria looked deeper into her house, to a safe space that Henk was suddenly certain he would never see again. When she turned back to face him, her eyes were soft, searching. "You're absolutely sure about this?"

For a moment, he almost said no, but he knew he would be failing himself if he stayed behind. There was nothing left for him here, especially with Maria apparently seeing the pig boy on the sly. The pill bottle pressed into his thigh, giving him the gentle nudge he needed. "It's no longer a choice."

Maria threw her arms around him. He reciprocated, burying his face in her hair and inhaling the aroma of her watermelon scented shampoo one last time. He told himself he would see her again soon. He then told Maria the same. Dave groaned as the rain switched directions and lashed down the back of his trainers. Henk reluctantly pulled away.

He didn't look back as they started up the long road towards the station. It would take at least an hour to get there on foot. They could have called a taxi—the temptation was strong given the treacherous weather. Henk couldn't put a finger on it, but something was telling him not to, that the fewer people knew they were leaving, the better.

Chapter 2

A dark front had rolled in by the time they made it to the station, reminiscent of the day they'd left town. Henk tossed a few notes at the taxi driver and dashed across the station's parking lot with fifteen minutes to spare. Dave was already inside, having rushed from the taxi after mumbling something about needing the toilet (an excuse to get out of paying his share of the fare, Henk assumed).

"What the hell is that?" Henk asked as Dave appeared with a stack of pre-packaged sandwiches.

"Dinner?" Despite his shorter-than-average size, Dave ate more than any one man should be able to. Henk had long since given up on trying to get him to eat normally. Dave was his own man, and Henk was hardly one to preach—he'd only ever consumed plain food and drinks for as long as he could remember. Dave tossed him a butter sandwich as they passed through the ticket barriers and boarded the end carriage of the grime-caked vehicle. A moment later, the train lurched away from the platform and rumbled out beneath the darkening skies in what was totally not a bad omen.

"Chill," Dave said around a mouthful of sausage and bacon. "You look like you're thinking about it again. How many times do I have to tell you all that superstition around the Head is baloney?"

He had *not* been thinking about *that* at all. In fact, *that* had been sequestered in the back of his mind and whipped until it was nothing more than an ethereal afterimage at the edge of his waking nightmares. But now it was scratching at the window, desperate for attention. He chewed his bread purposefully in an attempt to distract himself from the stoic features of the face in the field. The boulder-sized head, nestled in the damp grass and wrapped in large fingers. Eyes rolling back in their sockets like broken casino slots. It was *wheezing.*

A little after seven, the train screeched to a stop at Willow's Creek Station. The ride had been uneventful, and they seemed to have left the storm behind them, so Henk allowed himself to relax a little. It *would* be great to see Maria again after all this time, even if she *was* getting hitched to the asshole from the farm. Communication had been minimal when they first skipped town and had only dwindled rapidly after that. The rose-tinted glasses had come on heavy the first few weeks, and there were times, on particularly lonely nights, that he had been tempted to return. Not that he would ever allow himself.

But that seemed like a lifetime ago now. The catalysts that drove him from the town had softened over the years, downplayed and shrugged off the way one may when remembering the time they saw a shadow figure in the corner of their bedroom as a child.

And all it had taken was one sheet of card; one small note written in loopy cursive was all it had taken to reel him back in. Barely even personalised.

"Come on then!" Dave called from the steps at the end of the quaint platform—little more than several rows of rotten planking and a set of steps at the far end. "I thought you were having a stroke for a minute."

Henk surprised himself by laughing. The wooden boards creaked with thinly veiled malice as he trudged to the end of the platform. "Just bringing back memories is all."

"Oh yeah? Remember that whacky shit we used to smoke? What did we call it, mo-gro?"

"I'm not touching that shit again," Henk said.

"I sure as hell am. I'm not sitting through an entire wedding service without getting at least a little baked."

Henk grunted. The high from mo-gro was not worth the rest of the side effects, most of the time.

They left the station (if you could class the place as one) and scanned the road outside. No sign of a taxi, or anyone else for that matter. He removed his phone from his shirt pocket and checked the time. Had he read the invite wrong somehow? Unsurprised, yet still a little annoyed at the lack of service, they were now faced with a long walk.

What was he thinking anyway? He didn't want to watch his life-long crush marry someone else. He was about to tell Dave it might be for the best that their ride had failed to show when a set of dim headlights appeared in the distance. It looked as if the bulbs were straining, about to blow, and as it drew closer it became clear the lights were the least of its problems.

The battered Vauxhall Nova was the colour of piss-soaked sand. Incredibly front-heavy, the suspension groaned as the brakes slowed it with a drawn-out scream. Dave looked to Henk as the driver's window lowered, and a forearm as wide as a bucket flopped out, beckoned them closer. "Here for Maria?"

"Uh, yes."

"Hop on in. Bags in the boot."

With no better alternative, Henk popped the trunk and, after shoving aside several bags of fertilizer to make room for their belongings, climbed into the back of the car. Something hissed and scurried away as he reached for his seatbelt. He decided he'd rather chance not wearing one. The car groaned as Dave hopped in the other side, his face pinched upon coming into contact with the moist cushions. Then, with the tact of a crippled deer, said: "Christ, dude, you ever heard of deodorant?"

Henk died a little inside. Peering through the dark, musky interior of the car, a pair of bulging eyes stared back at him in the rear-view mirror. He was about to apologise for his brother's insensitivity when the man up front started laughing. The entire vehicle rocked in time with his whooping. "We got us a funny one!" The driver fumbled the interior light, illuminating his impressive mass.

All six hundred pounds of it. A bloated mess of jiggling meat that stretched from floor to roof, barely contained within the metal chassis like a tin of bloated spam. His size was the reason it had appeared so dark inside the car, blotting out most of the ambient light from the evening sky. An old-fashioned driving cap was wedged between the roof and the nub of semi-buried skull that was the man's head. A moss-green t-shirt was stretched across his sizeable bulk, split in several places across the back of his shoulders from which discoloured lumps of his dark skin bulged. The man's size was inconceivable. It defied logic. "What you're smelling back there is Poppy."

"Well, Poppy needs a bath," Dave muttered.

The driver's bulk shifted to display a broad smile and a set of uneven teeth. He flicked the light off, crunched the Vauxhall into gear and peeled away from the curb.

"Would you mind thinking before you speak for once?" Henk whispered. "The last thing I want is to piss this guy off while we're stuck in the back of his car."

"You're right. He is a bit of an ogre, isn't he? And what was that about Poppy? Smells like death. Probably still got her head in the glovebox."

If the driver heard anything Dave said, he gave no reaction.

Henk glared at Dave. Whether Dave could see his brother's expression was anyone's guess as they bounced down the first of many unlit country roads. The infrastructure surrounding the town had never been exceptionally well maintained but seemed to have gotten far worse since they'd been gone. Trying to look anywhere but at the man up front, Henk rubbed a layer of dust from the window with the sleeve of his jacket and tried to see if he could make out anything vaguely familiar as the scenery trundled by on a faulty conveyor belt. The darkness was suffocating, causing him to give up almost immediately and turn his head to the sky, which was just as awe-inspiring as he remembered. The blanket of shimmering lights reassured him that they weren't currently stuck in some kind of self-inflicted purgatory and were, in fact, still very much alive.

Dave farted. "Sorry. I thought it was going to be silent."

Henk moved to roll his window down but found the handle was missing. The driver paid little attention, whistling some long-forgotten show tune while thrumming his mighty paws on the steering wheel. Henk somehow doubted the man would even care if they both laid a log right there in the back of his car, given the current blend of scents fumigating the tin box. "So, you boys visited our little town before?" he said suddenly.

"We lived here, actually. A little while back," Henk said.

"That so?"

"Yeah. Went to college with Maria."

The driver shoved a finger into his ear canal, dug around. "Two Trees?"

"You know another one?"

"Used to work at Two Trees. Don't remember you folk, though. And I never forget a face," he said before extracting his finger and shoving it between his lips with a revolting sucking sound.

Dave, who had been trying to place the man while listening to the conversation unfold, shot up in his seat and clicked his fingers. "Jenk! I knew you sounded familiar. You've been working on that hockey body pretty hard, huh."

19

Henk would have bet money on the driver being anyone *but* Theobald Jenk, the school caretaker. Jenk had been a miserable young man that spent as much of his time jacking off in the supply cupboard as he did cleaning. A string bean of a man, the polar opposite of the guy up front.

"You remember me?" Jenk asked, attempting to turn his head to one-eighty but only succeeding in making the vehicle swerve violently to the left. Once he'd managed to correct it, he said: "Yeah, that's me. Used to bust a nut for that place and never got any recognition. I'd be lying if I said I wasn't at least a little happy when it started falling apart."

"What happened?" Dave asked. Henk, in all honestly, couldn't have cared less, but at least the conversation was helping the journey pass a little faster.

"Nothing too serious. Soggy ceiling here, loose window there. Problem was they never got anyone in to fix it up, and the place was eventually shut down. Didn't have the kids to justify it staying open by then, anyhow. These days, those that pop out runts either homeschool 'em, or put them straight to work. Easier on the town."

Henk spoke before Dave chimed in and took the conversation off into an entirely different tangent. "The college is gone?"

"Not exactly. It's still there, but it's condemned."

Henk was thrown from his seat as the car hit a pothole, almost cracking his head on the roof. A cloud of dust plumed into the musky air as he landed, intensifying the smell of aged meat. When he righted himself, there was light off to the left side of the road in the distance. The first sign of life. His old life. A cold tingle travelled up the back of his spine as a large wooden structure came into view through a gap in the hedgerow, and a tall figure carrying an axe could be seen lumbering toward a tied-up pig. A moment later, his view was obscured by the bushes. He stared intently at the staggered shrubbery and watched as the figure brought the blade down on the pig's neck in stop-motion.

"Ooh," Dave winced, having witnessed the butchery too. The pig's legs kicked for a moment, its corpse spinning weakly in the dirt. "Hey, Jenk? Is that farm still owned by the Notabaddie's?"

"Sure is. Got a few extra hands working for 'em now. Imagine they'll be cashing Poppy's ticket anytime."

It took a moment for the cogs to fall into place. If Poppy was the pig's name, it explained the smell in the back of the car. Henk shifted uncomfortably, wary of what else may be lurking in the car. "You've had a pig back here?"

"Heck, had most the town in the back of this car one time or another. Probably even shuttled your parents round a time or two if they're still in town."

"They're still in town, but I hope you haven't had them in the back of this car," Dave said. "They died before we left."

The driver looked as if he were trying to adjust his cap. He was silent for a moment before saying: "Well. I'm real sorry to hear that, boys." He then resumed whistling as if dead parents hadn't just been mentioned. Henk wasn't surprised—if things were anything like they used to be in Sorrow, the inhabitants were more than familiar with death. The more he thought of it, the stranger it was there was anyone left at all. Henk considered presenting the question in a package that wouldn't come across too forward but gave up as soon as an alternative failed to arise. "Are people still killing themselves?"

The driver peered into his side-view mirror, pretending he hadn't heard.

He elaborated, "When we lived here, before, people were killing themselves with knives."

"Self-decapitation," Dave added helpfully.

"What did you say you boy's names were again?"

"Henk and Dave—"

"Dave Wolfe. Shit, it *is* you guys! Didn't recognise you, what with the beards and all. You must be doing pretty well for yourselves now, huh?"

"Uh, sure."

"The town owes the two of you a whole lot more than whatever they're paying, you ask me. Lord knows how many people are in your debt."

The first of many buildings came into view ahead. The moon broke through a thick blanket of cloud cover to vomit a sickly glow across the cracked roof tiles of the post office as it rattled past. Time had not been kind to it, its windows darker than sin.

Next came the town hall, which by the looks of the sunken roof had long since shut, and a small shop that stocked anything from cigarettes to firewood. The driver took them down a series of winding roads into the town proper, eventually slowing as they entered Rookery Road. Here, the houses were modest and set back from the road just enough to not spill their light.

Crooked solar lamps along the front of several lawns broke up the oppressive gloom and gave the effect of a hellish landing strip.

The car grumbled to a halt in front of a squat building. The front garden was overgrown and littered with decorative windmills, many of which were bent at awkward angles. The house itself looked relatively inviting (although anywhere away from the mountain of a man was preferable at this point), and a soft amber glow peeked from the sides of several blinds.

Henk excused himself from the vehicle as quickly as possible, thankful for the fresh air. Dave took a little longer to emerge. "Making friends?" Henk asked as the car sputtered its way back up the road.

"I was asking what he meant by 'whatever the town's paying us'."

"And?"

"All he said was he was surprised we hadn't come back sooner to milk the cash cow."

"Forget about him," Henk said as he started down the short path to the house, "maybe his weight isn't the only thing that's slipped since we left."

"You're probably right. What was up with that? You'd need the jaws of life to get him out of there."

Henk was about to respond when he was interrupted by the sound of a lock being thrown. "Right. Behave yourself."

Maria looked exactly as Henk remembered. Wavy pink hair that kissed her shoulders the way a mother would kiss a newborn, eyebrows shaved in the shape of two small sausage dogs, and a perfect, baby-bearing figure. She wore a sparkly silver top and cut-off jean shorts that accentuated her long legs.

"Henkthaniel! And . . . how nice. Hello, David."

"Hi, Maria!" Dave beamed, ignoring her less than enthusiastic reception. "Pig-fucker home?" Maria's temperament never wavered despite the insult to her partner of so many years. If there needed to be anything else that Henk admired about her, it was that it was impossible to put her down. Maria would be in a good mood no matter the weather. It made her easy to be around.

"Harman is home, yes. He's tending to the Koi in the garden. Won't you both come in?" she asked, stepping aside and extending an arm to the warm interior.

Maria's parent's place was almost exactly as Henk remembered. Everywhere he looked were memories. The little reading nook under the staircase where they spent winter afternoons crammed on the single armchair together reading comic books. The black slate hearth around the fireplace that almost broke Dave's back, he'd struck it after a drunken handstand. They moved further through, to the back of the house, to the kitchen. The pantry door was ajar; another memory surfaced. They'd hid from Dave in there, giggling in the dark, and she'd suggested they pretend to kiss when he gets near, to freak him out when he discovered them. Although nervous, he'd been about to place his lips against hers when Dave threw the door open and interrupted. Not a week passed that he didn't think of that moment since. Had that moment been significant in how the rest of his life played out? He'd exhausted every avenue of thought over the years.

"A lot of memories in this house," he said as Maria handed him an open bottle of beer.

"Remember the time I literally scared the piss out of you, Henk?" Dave smirked, setting the bar for conversation low. "Remember? When I grabbed your foot as you were going up the stairs, and you pissed yourself?"

Maria giggled, taking it all in good humour. "Yes, I'm sure he remembers that, Dave. Mum spent an hour blotting it out of the carpet." Then, seeing Henk was uncomfortable, she asked: "How was the journey? I was a little worried you weren't coming when I didn't get an RSVP."

Henk peeled his lips away from the bottle. "Sorry about that. Was surprised to hear from you after all this time, if I'm honest. Thought you would have forgotten all about us by now."

"Are you kidding me?" Maria leant in for another hug. Henk's legs melted a little. "I'd never forget you." She pulled away and narrowed her eyes at Dave, "and I could never forget *you* now, could I."

Dave raised his beer and winked. "What's the deal with Jenk? He's really let himself go, hasn't he?"

"He's a silly man. After the school closed, he started working as a transporter. People, animals, goods, you name it. Not many cars around here anymore."

"Either way, I think he'd benefit from giving the driving a break. Stretch his legs a little." Dave knocked back the rest of his beer and immediately requested another.

The boys followed Maria across the hall to the study and took a seat across from her on a dark green leather sofa lined with gold studding. Bookshelves lined the walls, and a small desk was nestled in one corner, with a lamp emitting a soft golden glow. Across from the sofa were a set of sliding glass doors that led out to the back garden.

Henk found he'd finished his second beer before he'd even sat down, considered asking for a glass of water. He needed to pull himself together. They'd only arrived minutes ago, and already he was losing the confidence he'd spent the last years building up. Perhaps if he could get a moment alone with Maria, he could gently probe at her relationship with Harman.

A massive black shape appeared on the other side of the sliding patio door.

"Honey," Harman said as he let himself inside, a clear bag of fish flakes clasped in his right hand, "Why didn't you tell me we had guests? I would have cleaned myself up a little." Harman was sporting a massive gut held in place behind a set of muddy denim dungarees. His ginger hair was pulled into a tight bun at the back of his head, which accentuated the thick mutton chops on either side of his face. To Henk's surprise, the man was smiling, and his dolphin-blue eyes seemed to radiate genuine warmth.

"The boys just arrived, darling. I told you I'd invited them, remember?"

"Right," Harman said, his eyes narrowing as if trying to place the pair. He moved to shake their hands, but Dave pulled his away at the last second and left him hanging. Harman simply scrunched his face as if looking at an inquisitive animal. "Pleasure to see you both."

"Darling," Maria said, craning her head up to look at him as he stood beside her chair. "You *do* remember Henkthaniel and Dave?"

Harman placed a filthy fingernail to his lips in an exaggerated thoughtful pose. "Course I remember you two. How couldn't I?" he beamed, and for a moment, Henk thought he was about to have his hair rustled. "Honey, mind if we have a word in the kitchen for a moment? I need to find somewhere to put this." He held the fish food away from his body as if it were about to explode.

"Put it in the sink for now. I'll find a home for it later."

"I'd still like a word," he said, the smile never leaving his face.

Maria excused herself and followed her fiancé back to the kitchen.

"What was that about?" Henk whispered, looking around the room suspiciously as if they may be on camera.

Dave got up and started walking around the study, pulling out and replacing books for no real reason. "What do you mean? He's just screwing with us. I knew he'd do something like this. Good thing we didn't get them a wedding gift."

"I don't know, man. Don't you think he seemed different? Like, he seemed genuinely pleased to see us. I've never seen him look like that."

"Dude. Ten years is a long time. Sure, people change, but he's probably just rubbing in the fact he's been bumping nasties with the girl you fancied for the better part of your life."

"I'm not convinced. Something doesn't feel right."

"Will you knock it off with that shit? We're only here for a few days. Let's just try and have some fun."

Henk knew his brother was right. It was clear that the town still held the same power over him now as it had all those years ago. He told himself that he was going to be in control this time. Fuck the Head, and whatever weird shit was going on with the rest of the town—it wasn't his problem anymore. Maybe it wouldn't be such a bad idea to try and find some mo-gro. It had been a long time since he'd touched the stuff, but it sure would take the edge off.

Maria's perfect fucking face peered around the doorway. "More beer?"

"Love another," Dave said. Henk offered a weak smile and a thumbs-up, then kicked himself for being so dorky. He had small hands, not something he ever gave any particular thought or care to, but whenever he raised his one-inch thumb, it was hard to ignore. Maria returned promptly with two fresh bottles and her fiancée.

"Sorry about that, boys," Harman said, wiping his hands down the front of his dungarees. "It's been a while, hasn't it? You look so different. Henk, with that plaited Viking beard, and you, Dave, with all those fancy tattoos all over your arms. I was used to seeing you guys as teens."

Henk noticed Harman's smile now appeared strained. "No harm done. All set for the wedding?"

"Yes, we can't wait, can we, honey?" Harman slumped into the armchair next to Maria and smacked a meaty paw onto her knee. "We should go out for a drink this evening. Catch up."

Dave belched. "I'm game."

"I wouldn't mind a couple more," Henk agreed.

"Great. Let me get changed, and we'll head out."

After Harman clomped out of the room, Henk leaned forward and said, "Can I ask you something without you thinking I'm weird?"

Maria's eyes sparkled. "Henk, I've always thought you were weird. It's one of the things I like about you."

Henk felt blood rushing to his cheeks. "Are you two happy?"

The question surprised him even as it came out of his mouth. He was aware it was a wildly inappropriate question to pose, but years of repressed emotion were already breaking free of the cage from which he'd sequestered them. All it had taken was a few beers.

"Woah, man!" Dave chuckled, clapping his hands on Henk's shoulders from behind and giving a squeeze. "The lady's getting married in a few days. Bit late for that, isn't it?"

29

"No, sorry. I didn't mean it like that," Henk said, flustered. "I meant like, in the past, he never seemed like the kind of person we would have liked."

Maria's nose wrinkled. Henk could tell she was choosing how to word her answer carefully. "Perhaps," she said after what seemed like an eternity. "But that was all a long time ago."

"Of course." Henk stood and stretched dramatically. "Toilet still in the same place?"

Maria smiled, nodded.

Henk wandered down the hallway, cursing himself silently. He didn't need to piss at all—would rather wait before he broke the seal—but he needed a minute alone to pull himself together. He was almost at the bathroom when he heard Harmon muttering something, hushed tones reverberating from the front room.

"Never thought they'd come back. I told her they would be better off left alone. How am I supposed to trust her with him *here?"*

Heart pounding, Henk approached the doorway and peered through the crack in the door. He wasn't the type to eavesdrop, but when he was the subject of conversation, he could not stop himself.

A floorboard creaked further down the hall, back the way he'd come. "Forget where the bathroom is?" Maria asked, a playful lilt to her voice. Henk lowered his head and laughed it off as he made his way to the door across the hall.

The bathroom was like walking into a mirrored hell. No classic white wall tiles here, instead the walls were covered in sparkling silvery abominations. It was an epileptic's nightmare, yet it still failed to distract him from what he'd just heard moments before. Henk stood in front of the bowl for a moment longer before flushing and washing his hands. When he stepped back into the hallway, the others were waiting by the front door. Harman seemed to be having trouble meeting his eye.

Chapter 3

They'd barely made it out the front door when they came across the Gimp.

"What the fuck is that?" Dave said, pointing further up the road to a shimmering black outline moving through the shadows.

"The Gimp," Maria said matter-of-factly. "Every town has one!"

"Uh, I don't think that's quite right," Henk said. Then, "Who is it?"

Harman spoke up, quick to shut the conversation down: "Not sure. They don't cause any trouble, so we don't pay them any mind. Isn't that right, Maria?"

Maria nodded cheerfully.

Henk was expecting Dave to say something outrageous as the skinny leather-clad figure turned the corner at the end of the road, but to his surprise, he didn't. Perhaps he was catching up with the age of acceptance. If someone wants to walk around the place in a skintight suit with comical red rubberized lips, who were they to question it?

Henk spent the journey expecting it to jump out at them at any minute, but nothing happened. The only sign of life were a few crows fighting over a fox carcass and a large brown barn owl that watched on from the safety of a withered tree limb. Most of the houses they passed were void of life, with many looking as if they hadn't been lived in for quite some time.

The Swallow Inn was a welcome sight after what felt like a rather charged journey, and Henk was looking forward to getting another beer in him. Crunching across the gravelled parking lot (empty) towards the single-story building, he took a moment to appreciate the place's aesthetic. The thatched roof and Tudor-style windows were something he'd never really noticed before. It was only since moving to the city, surrounded by drab greys and browns, that he realized how lucky they had been to grow up in such a quirky area. The Inn sat on the edge of the town square. Opposite, across a vast expanse of grass, was a large building—Two Trees College.

It was a shadow of its former self: a slumbering behemoth, a rotten tooth right at the heart of the town. Parts of the roof appeared to have collapsed, windows were smashed, and the wooden extension on the left side had burnt down.

"Christ," Dave said.

"Christ indeed," Henk said. Then, to Maria, "Why has no one demolished it?"

"There's still hope it'll be open again one day. We get plenty of visitors now, but few people want to live here. I think it's been kept in the hope that may change."

Dave cocked an eyebrow at Henk, muttered, "At least my shit might still be there."

Henk ignored the comment. "Did something happen after we left? I mean, no offence, but Sorrow has never been the kind of place you'd want to holiday."

Maria giggled. "Of course not. It's still the same place it used to be. Sure, it might not be for everyone, but we have enough going on here now to bring in business."

Harman nodded in agreement, held the door open for Henk to lead the way inside.

Henk was greeted by the twin barrels of a well-used shotgun.

The barmaid was carved out of granite. She wore stretched suspenders over a white shirt. The comically large smile on her face did little to detract from the fact she was sporting what was quite possibly the world's worst combover, nor the fact she'd almost turned Henk's face into space dust mere seconds ago.

"Evening, Heidi," Maria said as if being greeted by a shotgun was nothing unusual. "Four pints, please."

The barmaid stared until her left eye began to twitch. Only then did she break her gaze and leave to retrieve the glasses from the back shelf of the bar.

"Anyone for a game?" Harman offered, taking a couple of snooker cues off the rack and practically forcing one into Dave's hand.

"You're on, pig boy."

An old man sat hunched over a half-empty pint of black stuff, stinking of stale cigars and bad life choices. He lifted his head only once, and Henk thought he saw a glint of recognition in his eye. At some point, he hauled himself from the barstool and disappeared into the toilets.

One drink turned into three, into five. The entire time Heidi wore the stretched smile as if her cheeks were stapled. Maria said she imagined the woman had suffered some sort of stroke, and that the shotgun was merely a precaution, as it was generally not recommended to be out after dark. After almost falling over his own feet, Harman decided he'd had enough to drink and excused himself to head to bed. It could have been the alcohol, but the evening seemed to have gone quite well, and Henk decided he'd been too hasty in his wariness of the place, and his judgement of Harman. They were adults now. Not emotional teenagers caught up in fighting the forces of evil. What had he been so worried about? Of course, it helped that Maria had informed them the town had not suffered an attack from an entity in several years, though he got the impression she was holding something back.

Around ten-thirty Maria hugged the boys and told them to meet her in the town square in the afternoon, stating she had a big surprise. "You remember how to get to the hotel?" she slurred.

"Over the footbridge past the store. We'll be fine. You get back to your future husband," Henk said.

Dave slammed an open palm on the ring-stained table, almost knocking his glass to the floor. "Now get out of here before he declares his undying love for you."

Maria laughed. "All right, boys. Just head straight there, okay? Things might be better here, but that doesn't mean there isn't the odd weirdo about. See you tomorrow."

Now alone in the pub with the barmaid, they became even more aware of her unsettling gaze. "I'm going to take a piss," Dave half-shouted behind his hand, "then we're going back to school."

"You *still* want to do that? I don't think we should be going in there. The place is practically a textbook definition of danger."

"Danger is my middle name, baby."

Henk couldn't argue with that—Dave had legally changed his middle name to Danger a few years back after discovering how cheap it was to do so online. He polished off the last of his beer while waiting for his brother to come back, ran his fingers along the cracks in the wooden tabletop. Could they have sat at this very table with their parents when they were younger? Quite possibly, he supposed. Everything in the place looked about a hundred years old, from the thick oak beams running across the ceiling to the array of horseshoes tacked along the top of the bar.

Dave stumbled out of the toilet, beckoned Henk with his hand. "There's a headless guy in there," he called to the barmaid on their way out.

The crisp evening air was sobering. "Was there really a body in there?" Henk asked as they made their way across the car park.

"That guy that was at the bar earlier? It looked like he tried to decapitate himself with the toilet tank lid. Could at least have given a courtesy flush. It stank in there."

"It's still going on," Henk muttered.

It had been a long time since either of them had seen a corpse, yet it came as little surprise to either of them to find one so soon into their visit. Their lack of concern may seem a tad suspicious to the casual observer, but death was as much of a part of life as birth in the town, especially suicide. It was the main reason Henk had been so desperate to leave in the first place. At the time, he'd thought it was perhaps all in his head— that his glass-half-empty attitude may have been making things seem worse than they were. After this, he wasn't so sure. In fact, he was convinced that nothing had changed.

The town was cursed, and it all came back to the Head.

Chapter 4

After a quick lap of the college, Dave decided the best way in would be through one of the broken windows around the back. There was little fear of being caught, as they'd hardly seen anyone else since arriving in town. Henk hung back while Dave hopped onto the windowsill and peered into the gloom on the other side. A moment later, he was through, giggling to himself like a love-drunk schoolgirl. Henk had no choice but to follow.

"Place hasn't changed a bit," Dave said, toe-punting a semi-deflated football down the darkened corridor.

"Ignoring the obvious," Henk agreed. He pulled out his phone and activated the torch, tracing the beam along a tangle of ivy that had broken through a crack in the cement on a reclamation mission. The entire place smelled of rot. "Let's just grab your shit and get out of here. I'm tired, man."

Kicking the ball along the hallway ahead, they eventually reached class 4-C. The room was identical to the others, with a dust-streaked whiteboard at one end and a dozen or so desks facing it. A mess of mathematical equations were barely legible on the board. Dave dragged a chair over to the supply cabinet in the back corner of the room and climbed up to the air vent while Henk traced a smiley face in the layer of dirt on his old desk.

"Bingo!" Dave cried, thrusting the bag of mo-gro into the air as if it were an Olympic medal. "Looks kinda funky, though." He hopped to the floor with a bang, knocking over the chair in the process. He shook the baggie out to proudly display a cluster of glowing blue buds. Dave popped the seal and stuck his nose into the bag before throwing his head back with a dramatic exhale. "A good year. Aged like a fine wine."

Henk moved about the classroom, inspecting drawers and shelves until he heard a sparking sound behind him. The room glowed orange momentarily.

Dave coughed on the exhale, doubled over. When he stood upright, he was sporting a ridiculous grin. The skin of his face was already lifting in several places. He extended the joint to Henk, who hesitated. He'd been drug-free for several years at this point. He wasn't usually one to bow to peer pressure, either, but being back here (he tried to avoid thinking the term *home*), he could feel himself regressing to his youth. To a time he had fewer worries, with his whole life was ahead of him, an untapped fountain of opportunity.

Before their parents killed themselves.

Henk took the joint. This little trip had been a rollercoaster of emotion already. Perhaps this was precisely what he needed. He inhaled a slight puff to avoid choking on the musky herb, felt himself relax almost immediately. The sensation of movement beneath his skin was not one he had ever got used to—like an entire family of botflies were fighting to get out—but damn it felt incredible once they broke the surface. They finished the joint at their old desks, poking and prodding at the raised welts beneath their arms until the luminescent fingers pushed through their pores and breached the surface.

The first time they'd tried smoking the mo-gro, the fingers had freaked them the fuck out, with Henk even trying to wrench them out of him with a pair of pliers. But once they realized the wriggling blue flesh was a part of them, simply another side effect of the drug that would fade along with the high, it became something to experiment with more than anything else.

They were on their way out of the building when a scratching noise started up in a classroom further down the hall. "Should we check it out?" Dave said.

"No. Haven't you ever seen a horror movie?"

Dave turned back. "Don't be such a pussy."

The corridor was covered in crude, child-like graffiti. Above the door in question was a portrait of an upside-down stick person surrounded by fingers. Dave peered into the musky classroom, then whispered, "There's someone in there."

High for the first time in what felt like a lifetime, Henk's senses went into overdrive. Nothing good could come of this, a fact that the spasming fingers around his elbows seemed to agree with. He attempted to convey this to Dave without words but, Dave stepped over the threshold. "Miss Henning? Is that you? What are you doing?"

Matilda Henning was 'that' teacher. The one every boy in school had a crush on and imagined she got off on knowing it. She often wore a short black pencil skirt and a white shirt that barely contained her breasts, but management had eventually forced her to wear something that didn't cause the teens in her class to walk around with permanent tents in the front of their trousers. At least, that was Dave's hypothesis. Henk imagined it was more likely that she cottoned onto the fact she was being ogled and started covering up a little more under her own free will.

The woman stood with her back to them. One arm raised towards the whiteboard, frozen mid-stroke. The marker pen clasped between her fingers had worn down to nothing more than a nub; the only thing she'd been drawing were deep scratches in the board. There was something a little funny about the way she held herself, but it was hard to tell in the poor light. Miss Henning snapped towards the pair. Her dark hair swept across her face, arms fell loose, swinging at her sides as if every bone in them had just melted out of her fingertips. The marker pen clattered to the floor.

"Excuse us," Henk said, "We'll be going now."

Matilda swung an arm behind her and slapped it against the board with a loud *thwap*. Her other hand rose to point at the clock on the wall to their right, which was frozen at three-thirty and covered in enough cobwebs to stitch a scarf.

"I don't understand," Dave said. "You want to know the time?"

41

The teacher lowered her hand and cast it across the filthy desks across the floor of the room.

"Dave, let's go," Henk whispered as he started to back away.

Dave waved him off without looking at him. To the teacher, he said: "Are we late? Is that it? You want to teach us a lesson? Because I already know my math, and you have one *significant* figure."

"DAVE."

This time, Dave turned to face him. "Keep it down, man. I don't want to get spanked for talking in class."

Henk knew if he tried to leave right now, he would be going alone. He couldn't do that. Whatever that thing was, it wasn't Matilda Henning, and he wasn't about to leave Dave alone with it, no matter how forcefully his legs were urging him to sprint in the opposite direction. Instead, he picked up the nearest plastic chair and raised it over his head.

"The fuck, bro?" Dave said. His chair squealed as he pushed away from the desk. "I know it's been a while since you smoked, but-"

Henk wasn't listening. He stepped forward and threw the chair in the woman's direction as hard as he could. Dave ducked even though he was in no danger of being hit—the brittle projectile sailed over his head and exploded against the whiteboard.

Matilda Henning was gone.

There one moment, gone the next.

Dave picked himself up and looked to the front of the room. "Woah."

They approached the front of the dark classroom hesitantly and rounded the teacher's desk. There was nothing but a scorched crater of loose concrete roughly three feet across.

Dave clucked his tongue. "Fancy another smoke?"

Henk sighed. "Go on then."

Chapter 5

It was a little after midnight by the time the pair arrived at the hotel. A weather-worn sign proclaimed they'd reached "The Safest Place in Sorrow!" and another stated: "We'll KILL for Your Comfort!"

Henk released the gate latch and started up the path to the domineering modern building. Concrete pillars flanked the tall wooden door. Rows of windows stretched from floor to ceiling. The roof was arched into a peak that seemed to penetrate the night sky. It was a far cry from the building they'd been expecting to see—a cosy four-bed cottage had once stood in its place. Most windows were darkened, but the lobby was lit and shimmering thanks to a backlit indoor waterfall. A neon rainbow hovered over the water as it cascaded over rocks and pots before collecting in a large pool at the base. The entire place had an air of excessiveness. How many guests were they expecting to get out here?

They passed a winding staircase and approached a marble-topped desk at the rear of the lobby. Dave took a pamphlet from the plastic stand on the counter while Henk pressed the service bell.

"Welcome," said a disembodied voice. A moment later, a bald, thin man rose from behind the desk with a fistful of papers. He had a sharp, pointed nose and a thick monobrow that arched slightly as he spoke.

"Hi, Mort," Henk said.

The ex-mortician sized the pair up for a moment, his pale veins flexing beneath his thin skin. "The Wolfes. What a pleasure to see you again. How have you both been?" The man asked as he shuffled to a locked cabinet on the wall beyond the desk.

"Never better," Henk said. "Looks like you've been doing fairly well for yourself too."

"I am indebted to you as much as the rest of the town," Mort said over his shoulder.

"You're going to want to see this," Dave said without looking up from the colourful pamphlet. Henk decided whatever faraway attraction his brother wanted to show him could wait. Although the mo-gro had worn off (it usually lasted an hour or so), it was taking his full concentration to remain focused on the man approaching with the room key. Mort said something that Henk couldn't make out, but when he tried to hand him his card to pay for the booking, he waved him off, saying it was all paid up. He told them they would find their twin room on the second floor to the rear of the building.

"Seriously, Henk. Look at this," Dave said as soon as they were out of earshot. He thrust the unfolded paper in Henk's face.

For a moment, Henk forgot where he was, his eyes glued to the pompous cursive at the top of the page. "No fucking way."

Welcome to the World of Sorrow!
Do you want to enjoy a NEAR-DEATH EXPERIENCE?
VISIT SORROW!

MATTHEW A. CLARKE

Do you ever get the feeling you're being watched? How about a gnawing sense of hopelessness? Or perhaps you're simply curious about the world beyond our own and wish to visit the home of nature's finest curiosity for yourself.

VISIT SORROW!

Founded in 1546, the villagers of Sorrow settled in a remote location in the English countryside with the hopes of building a self-sustaining society that would stand the test of time. With an abundance of wood, wildlife, and clean, flowing water, what could possibly go wrong?

Fast-forward to 1712, and a band of weary travellers stumbled upon the town to find every inhabitant had either decapitated themselves or gone insane. Isn't that COOL?! Sorrow has seen calmer times and a thriving trade lumber in the modern day, yet there is no denying that the otherworldly presence is still all around!

Do you want an experience you'll never forget? Perhaps you'd like to learn more about the strange entities that our townsfolk have defeated? Why wait?

People are DYING to learn more!

UNDER NO CIRCUMSTANCES SHALL THE TOWN OF SORROW, ITS INHABITANTS, BUSINESSES, OR PARTNERS BE LIABLE FOR ANY DIRECT, OR INDIRECT, INCIDENTAL, CONSEQUENTIAL, SPECIAL, OR EXEMPLARY DEATH OR HARM BROUGHT TO VISITORS. WHETHER OR NOT THE HARM AND/OR DEATH WAS FORESEEABLE, THE TOWN AGGREGATES LIABILITY TO YOU.

"They turned this place into some kind of morbid tourist attraction."

"Looks that way," Dave said, scratching his handlebar moustache. "I can't see what anyone would find interesting in this town, though."

Henk raised an eyebrow but wasn't sure it was worth the response. The things people had been saying to them were starting to make a little more sense.

Their room was modest but more than they really could have hoped for; twin beds, soft pillows, and a couple of foil-wrapped chocolates on a coffee tray. As Henk moved to close the curtains, he saw a familiar figure skating through the shadows.

The Gimp froze as if it knew it was being watched.

Henk turned his back and crawled into bed.

Chapter 6

A pounding at their door.

It was still dark out, and Henk threw the covers off and checked the time. Five-thirty a.m. He looked over to Dave and saw he was still sound asleep, a thin trickle of drool leaking from the corner of his open mouth.

He stood and moved to the door.

"Henk! I'm so sorry. I didn't know where else to go," Maria said, mascara running down her face and giving the impression her sausage dog eyebrows were suffering from diarrhea.

"Slow down," he said, his fogged brain struggling to process. "What's going on?"

"It's Harman. He wasn't home when I got back last night. I haven't slept. I don't know where he could be."

"Calm down." Henk turned on the light, thankful he wasn't suffering from morning wood. He then moved to the bathroom's little sink, cupped his hands, and filled them with cold water. "Has he ever done this before?"

"No. Never. I'm worried something's happened to him."

"I suppose it's a good thing we're here then," Henk said as he approached Dave's bed and hurled the cold water onto his face, causing him to jolt awake with a cry.

Dave swung his legs out of bed, instantly alert. "The old gang's getting back together?!"

Henk waited tensely for Maria's response. Her fingers grasped anxiously at the hem of her jacket. "I suppose it is."

After successfully capturing the Wailing Widow with nothing more than a few mirrors and a punji pit, the trio had solved their first 'case' at the age of twelve. The entity had been terrorising the town for weeks before they decided to step in and put an end to her spooky shenanigans. Utterly terrified of mirrors, the cantankerous old hag had been breaking into people's homes and smashing every reflective surface.

Maria's house was an obvious target for the Wailing Widow. Her mother shared Maria's passion for all things glittery, making their house a homing beacon for the menace. The trio had hidden in the bushes outside every night for almost a week until she eventually showed. They'd leapt out and used mirrors to back her into the dug-out pit on the front lawn. The townsfolk were happy with the Widow turning up dead—she wasn't exactly human. As long as she was out of the picture, the details didn't matter.

And so began the dawn of a new era for the town of Sorrow. At least in the kid's eyes. Investigating the curiosities that had a habit of sprouting kept them out of trouble and gave them a sense of purpose, something to live for.

Then, the brother's parents had died, the latest in an ongoing string of bizarre suicides, and Henk was able to see the town for what it really was.

An irredeemable cesspit of unhappiness.

"I've been waiting so long for this," Dave said, practically tripping over himself to get out the door.

"Relax," Henk said. "We're not kids anymore. We're looking for Harman, not trouble."

"For you, maybe."

"Whatever." He lowered his voice as Dave started performing lunges in the hall outside their room. "I'm sorry, Maria. Ignore him. I'm sure we'll find Harman without any problem. Any idea where we should start?"

She looked to the ceiling and sucked in her lower lip. "I suppose we could check his father's place. I'm not sure why he would have gone there in the middle of the night, but I'm having trouble figuring out why he would have gone *anywhere*."

"The farm just outside of town, yes? Sounds like a good idea as any."

"Come ON, you guys!"

Henk locked the room, then the three of them made their way back down to the lobby. Mort was nowhere to be seen, but the pamphlets on the desk caught his eye once more. "How come you didn't mention this place had become a tourist attraction?" he asked Maria.

"I assumed you would have heard already. We've become quite famous in this neck of the woods. Who would have thought?"

"Macabre tourists," Dave said.

"Uh-huh." Maria perked up, a little light returning to her bottomless blue eyes. People love seeing dead bodies. Murder sites. I love that the place we grew up in is getting some long-overdue recognition, but I think the rest of it is just pure silliness."

"The stuff about the Head?" Henk asked.

"Yup. Bunch of mumbo jumbo if you ask me! I've never felt any such thing. I think people that kill themselves were going to do it with or without 'psychic interference' from that thing." Maria placed a hand on Henk's pectoral, and like a chest paddle, it sent shockwaves through his heart. "Oh, God. I'm so sorry. I didn't mean-"

"That's okay. You're probably right anyway."

Maria let her gaze linger on him a moment longer than perhaps necessary. Her own parents had died a few years back in a road traffic collision with a fuel transport lorry on a motorway. It wasn't the initial crash that killed them, but the fireball that followed. However, it didn't seem like the time to mention it, and they hadn't asked. "I guess I thought you might have wanted to stay away if you knew Sorrow's history was being celebrated instead of respected. I remember how you were struggling, and I guess I thought you might have been angry that people were profiting off it."

"If people want to risk their lives visiting this shithole, let them. No skin off my nuts."

"It's really not that bad anymore. If it was, I wouldn't have invited you back, would I?"

By the time they reached the town's outskirts, the sun had breached the horizon, staining the sky a pale pink-yellow, the colour of infection. The first of the morning commuters could be heard over the hills. Horns bleeting wearily from overuse, stressed folk rushing to get to work, to spend their day watching the clock, before rushing to get back home again. On the main road in and out of town, the only thing stirring was the wildlife. Foxes scurried through brambles, fleeing the rising sun to the safety of their underground homes. Magpies took flight to begin a busy day of brainless circling. A lone hedgehog watched them pass from inside a chewed-up cardboard box.

"We're here," Maria said.

Notabaddie farm prospered along with the rest of the town. As the sole producer of meat and vegetables for the surrounding areas for as long as anyone could remember, the increased visitor numbers had necessitated a ramping up of production, and, in turn, funded larger buildings and slightly-more-modern machinery, all of which required additional hands to keep the place running smoothly. Henk slapped a hand across Dave's chest as a dark figure crossed the dirt track outside a red cattle barn. The figure was formless, even in the growing light.

"Relax," Maria said. "They're harmless. Jeff took them on to help around the farm after we killed the Spectre. They're free labour and relatively docile without their master around."

Dave ran off ahead laughing. He intercepted the Shade and drew circles with his hand inside its ethereal body. "You've got to be shitting me! I thought we banished all of these guys!" Maria walked ahead, leaving Henk to compose himself a little. He wondered how much help a Shade could be in a job that typically consisted of manual labour.

Maria slapped Dave's hand out of the Shade's chest, pulled him away by the wrist. She then addressed Henk as if reading his mind, "They're used for herding the animals."

Henk wished he could adjust to the once-evil creatures walking around freely as easily as his brother. He could understand Maria being unphased, but Dave had run ahead to tease it without a second thought, unperturbed by the fact one of them had almost syphoned his soul from his eyes the last time they crossed paths. What else had changed around here? Was this the key to living a happy life in the Sorrow? Instead of fighting the evils that rear their ugly heads, why not try to embrace them? Treat it like a culture? It seemed to be working out okay for everyone else, bar the occasional murder spree. But he still couldn't shake the feeling that they'd been lured into a false sense of security, that something was biding its time, waiting for the opportune moment to strike.

There was no fucking way he was letting his guard down. Even if everyone else was happy to keep their heads down, live in ignorance of the dangers to live a more content (albeit potentially shorter) existence, Henk was not going to be one of them.

But if Harman didn't show? He was a little disgusted at himself for feeling a twinge of hope that he may still have a chance with the One that Stayed Behind. Then again . . . if his previous experience of Sorrow were anything to go by, it would not be prudent to proceed without a contingency plan. Would Harman's unexplained disappearance be enough to get Maria to leave Sorrow once and for all and live a happy (if not humble) life with him in the city? A guy could dream.

"Henk? Hey, Henk!" Dave was bent over the metal rungs at the front of the cattle barn getting his face licked by a large cow.

The further they progressed onto the farmland, the more run down it became. Rusted tractors lay alongside burnt-out caravans, both doors and glass missing, replaced by thick ropes of thistle and nettles. A cracked metal barrel lay on its side, the contents burnt and spilt across the path. Blackened bones lay among the ashes, too small to be human but too large to be your typical barbecued meats. By the time they approached the cottage, they were practically wading through a mound of discarded plastic, newspaper, and an unimaginable amount of animal faeces.

Henk kicked aside a washing machine drum. "Is this normal?"

"Jeff has trouble getting around these days. Harman usually takes care of the tip runs for him. I guess it's been a little longer than I realised since he last came up this way." Maria stooped to pick up a rubber dog toy before throwing it over her shoulder and muttering to herself. "Doesn't even have a dog." She then approached the front door of the cottage and knocked twice. After waiting a few moments, Dave moved along the side of the building and peered into one of the darkened windows. The glass was cracked but still just about clinging onto life.

"Place is a dump," he said.

Maria joined him. "What on earth? How could he have let it get this untidy?"

Untidy was an understatement. The wooden floor was lifted in several places. Furniture broken, perhaps tossed with ill intent. Here, a splintered coffee table, there, a shattered chair. From the marks on the walls, it looked as if something had worked its way up the wall in the far back corner and pushed through to the upper floor. Whatever it was that did it was gone. Henk tried the front door. Locked. "We need to get in there."

Maria called Jeff's name while knocking gently on the window. The glass shattered under her touch, cascading into the room like a thin sheet of ice. She leapt back and checked her knuckles for splinters. Dave shrugged. "Guess we've got our way in." He led the way, climbing cautiously to avoid cuts, followed by Maria, then Henk. Somehow, the room smelled even worse than it looked. It was as if a skip full of garden waste had been left in a dog's arsehole to ferment.

"Jeff?" Maria called again. Henk wasn't surprised that there was still no response. If a broken window wasn't enough to bring him running, Maria's voice was unlikely to do the job. "This is Harman's," she said, crouching to pick up a

55

leatherbound wallet. She slipped it into the front pocket of her jeans. "He must have come here . . ."

The rest of the cottage was in a similar state of disrepair. In the kitchen, cupboards hung open, and plates lay smashed across the chipped tiles. Upstairs, in the master bedroom, the double bed was bowed upward in the middle as if something had struck it from beneath. Although the house remained quiet, Henk swore he could hear a faint rustling.

"No. This isn't right at all," Maria confirmed as if the others needed any convincing.

"What now?" Henk asked.

Maria looked lost for a moment, her hands forming fists at her sides. Then, as if a switch had been thrown, she brightened, nodded once so sharply that her hair swung across her shoulders. "The church. It's the only other place that makes any sense." Maria turned and made her way back downstairs with a big smile on her face.

"Dave," Henk said, lowering his voice in the hope Maria wouldn't hear. Dave pulled his attention from the bubbled wallpaper he had been prodding. "Does Maria seem a little off to you?"

"Cut her some slack, man. The guy she's supposed to be marrying has gone missing. Besides, she's always been a little," he placed a finger against his temple and rolled his eyes. "She's way too hot to have been friends with us if she wasn't."

Dave had a point. Maria had been the best-looking girl at their school by a long shot. However, her eccentricities tended to turn off most potential suitors, which meant Henk had never had to deal with her being taken away by a boyfriend.

"Hold up," Henk said as they reached the front door. "Look."

Across the front room was a small door they hadn't noticed on the way in, half-covered by a fallen bookcase. Dave crossed the room and walked the bookshelf away from the wall.

"That's the basement," Maria said, making Henk physically jump. He'd been so engrossed in the hidden door that he hadn't noticed her coming up alongside him. "It's where Jeff dries the meats."

"It's unlocked," Dave said, pulling it and waving away a string of cobwebs that stretched across the opening.

The door led onto a narrow set of stairs. A hanging pull switch did nothing when pulled, but a series of small holes in the ceiling marked the way ahead. Reaching the bottom of the stairs, they found the concrete floor covered in a thin layer of water, as if a pipe had ruptured somewhere unseen. A thick ventilation duct ran the length of the cracked wall and disappeared into the ceiling. They moved toward a light at the far end, past racks of thinly sliced meats and large animal carcasses on hooks until the floor beneath their feet began to crumble and break away. "He's not down here," Henk said. "We're wasting time."

"Jeff?" Maria called. "What are you doing?"

After a moment, Henk noticed a man, an older-looking Harman, standing below eye level on what looked to be a collapsed section of the basement floor at least fifty metres away. The ground had given way and formed some sort of small canyon full of luminous blue . . . fingers. There was no doubt. Thick, impossibly long fingers were wrapped around Jeff's waist and neck, fading into the darkness behind him. Jeff's head was at an awkward angle, almost touching his left shoulder.

"Jeff," Maria continued, raising her voice. "Have you seen Harman?" The mass that was potentially Harman's father remained still. "I haven't seen him since last night. I don't think he came home."

Henk looked to his brother for confirmation that he wasn't the only one thinking the abnormally long digits were a little concerning. Dave exhaled dramatically. "Everything okay down there, dude?"

"I think we should go and get help," Henk said. "Who knows how stable the rest of this place is. He's clearly already dead. We could end up stuck down there with him if we're not careful."

Maria cupped her hands to her mouth and said, "If you're busy, we can come back later. I was just hoping you might have spoken to him, is all."

Dave rolled his shoulders. "Fuck that. We can handle this." He proceeded to grab a fistful of ivy and rip it free from the wall. "I'm going Tarzan on this bitch."

"Are you serious?" Henk started, but Dave was already taking a run-up, his hands wrapped around the organic mass. With a warbling howl, he threw himself off the lip of the basement floor and tucked his knees to his chest. Because he'd neglected to take into account the vines had initially sprouted from beneath the floor before working their way up to the ceiling, after the few seconds it took for them to tear away, he plummeted into oblivion.

Or so it appeared to the others. "Dave!" Henk ran to the edge of the broken floor section and peered over the edge to see Dave flat on his back on a cushion of crushed ivy. He raised both thumbs and began to laugh.

Maria called out to her future father-in-law once more. "We're coming for you! Just stay where you are."

Dave pulled himself to his feet and kicked away a finger the width of a cucumber that had been closing in on him.

"Oh, no," Maria whispered.

"Eh?" Henk said.

"Dave, I think it's too late. You need to come back up. Now."

Henk stared at her intently. "What's wrong?"

"I'm okay!" Dave called, his voice seeming to echo somewhere far away. Then, to Jeff, "Hang tight, mate."

Henk watched as the fingers shrank, retreating across the ceiling, then the walls. Before long, the ambient light they were giving off would be gone, and Dave would be left in the dark entirely. Henk activated his torch app, then told his brother to do the same.

After a slight pause, Dave moaned. "I think it broke in the fall."

"You need to get back up here *now*. It's too dangerous. Jeff's already dead."

Henk expected Maria to at the very least shoot him daggers, but instead, she agreed with him. "We'll have to come back for Jeff later, Dave."

"What do you mean?" came the response from the gloom. "He's right here . . . what the—"

"DAVE!" Henk shouted as Jeff's body was lifted slowly into the air. The fingers tightened around his wrists and ankles, snapping his limbs into unreasonable angles. His exposed skin bubbled and popped like fat on a fire, his clothing started to smoke.

"What're you doing up there?" Dave said to Jeff. "Screw this. I'm coming back up."

A few minutes later, safely regrouped, the trio stepped out into the fresh countryside air (thick with the smell of manure and smouldering bonfire, it still beat the hell out of whatever was stinking up the cottage). The Shades could be seen moving about the expanse of the fields to the left and right, herding sheep and cows, but there was still no sign of human life.

"I thought we'd seen the last of those things," Dave said, peeling a fingernail the size of a block of cheese from his trouser leg.

Henk gave Maria a moment to offer further explanation for what she had said down in the basement, but she was staring dreamily off into the distance. "Maria," he said gently.

She turned to face him, her eyes unfocussed. "Oh, I wouldn't worry about the fingers. They've been around for a while, but they don't seem overly dangerous, usually."

"You want to tell that to Jeff?"

Her eyes skittered. "Well, like I said, they're not usually."

Whatever Dave said in response was nothing but a muted buzzing to Henk as a lead balloon forced its way up his throat, a revelation hitting him like a fist to the temple.

It was the Head. It had to be connected. Despite his best efforts to think of literally anything else, the face started to form in his mind.

It was the size and shape of the moai, on Easter Island, only flesh and bone rather than volcanic rock. Eyes wide, white, rolling back marbles in their sockets. The tall anomaly was genderless, covered in dirt and bark, and insects. Its mouth was slightly ajar, and exhaling hard enough to suffocate Henk with its malodorous breath.

"Why now?"

"There he is," Dave said. "Welcome back."

"Why now?" he said again, this time mostly to himself. What if coming back to Sorrow was precisely what he needed to do? If he could put this bogey man to bed once and for all, perhaps he could finally move on with his life.

Dave kicked a rock towards an approaching Shade. "We've got a new case?"

Henk looked Maria in the eye and said, "You need to tell me everything you know about the fingers."

Chapter 7

The Head had been increasingly active over recent months.

On a drizzly New Year's afternoon, after following a pooh stick down the river that ran down the left-side of town, little Sally Ruther had practically run straight into the back of the Head. She'd rushed home to tell her parents, but by the time they'd returned to the site, it was gone. They'd brushed it off as nothing more than a child's active imagination, a cry for attention, that is until Pastor Wicker went to investigate the woods behind his house one night after his dog refused to settle. Something had been out there, something only the German Shepherd could sense. That something turned out to be the Head, and after cautiously approaching, it shot underground. As far as people familiar with the Head were concerned, it was not normal that it would allow anyone to get so close to it. It would usually sink into the ground if anyone got too close, only to crop up somewhere else almost instantly.

More recently, the fingers had started to appear.

They were great for business—it had been several years since the last spate of deaths, and tourism had been starting to wane. When the council first heard about this new development, they'd created an extensive advertising campaign in an attempt to bring some extra money into the town, and for the most part, it had worked. Parents brought children to participate in 'Hunt the Head' weekends, where the kids would get their faces painted with blue fingers and go out in packs to search for the elusive being. News reporters came by, hoping to scoop an exclusive with the Head (they were never successful), and religious fanatics flocked from around the globe, citing it to be a manifestation of whatever deity they chose to believe in.

But Henk wasn't having any of it. Growing up in Sorrow, he knew better than anyone that it was not a 'fun' place to visit and certainly not a safe, family-friendly weekend retreat, but it didn't stop the uninitiated from coming. For many, leading their dull nine-to-five lives, it was the thrill of danger that drew them in the first place. It could be likened to visiting a famous haunted location, in that it's unlikely that anything will happen in the time you're there, but knowing there is that chance can make an otherwise unassuming location far more exciting.

But what did this have to do with Harman's disappearance? Jeff Notabaddie was one of those that now belonged to the fingers, and his son's wallet was recovered from the scene. Maria seemed reluctant to admit it, but there was a good chance that Harman was gone too.

"So, what are we thinking?" Dave asked. "We find the Head and kick its ass?"

"It doesn't have an ass," Henk said.

Maria looked up from chewing the skin around her fingernails. "I don't exactly have time to go hunting monsters right now."

"You'll have plenty of time if we can't find the groom," Dave muttered.

"I suppose you're right."

They walked in silence for a few moments before Henk said, "I think we should go and see Pastor Wicker. If he was the last person to see the Head, he might be able to tell us something about the fingers we don't already know."

By the time they reached the rest of civilisation, the streets were bustling with life. Children walked hand-in-hand with their parents, white shirts with 'I Survived Sorrow!' printed across their chests in dripping red lettering. Young couples laughed and posed for selfies in front of shops and memorial benches to be uploaded to social media as soon as they returned to an area with reception (#sorrowsurvivor and #murdertown were often trending). Then, there were those that were all business—a popular destination for ghost hunters/wannabe detectives. You were never too far from a guy dressed in cargo trousers with stuffed pockets, and backpacks (presumably) full of all manner of electronic devices.

"This is so weird," Henk said.

"It's a quaint English town rich in history and forgotten by time," Maria said. "What's not to love?"

Before either could reply with a sarcastic comment, of which there were plenty, two young boys with matching Wailing Widow baseball caps screamed and pointed at them. "Mum!

Dad! They're back! It's the Sons of Sorrow!" Henk cringed at the nickname they'd given themselves as kids as the hyper boys peeled away from their guardians and charged towards the trio, thrust their pens and pads into their hands. "Please, can you sign our books? Please!"

Henk turned the paperback over in his hands and was greeted by the sight of his own face looking back at him. He raised the book to Maria. "Care to explain?"

Maria took the book and the pen from him, scrawled a signature on the inside page, then said, "We're somewhat famous around here. I guess when you guys left, you became local legends."

"Sweet!" Dave said. He high-fived the kids and scrawled his signature alongside Maria's—a cross-eyed smiley face.

Henk refused to take the book from his brother. "Sorry, kids. I'm no role model. Your parents have put you in serious danger bringing you here and should be ashamed of themselves."

The twins looked up at Henk for a moment with wide, anime eyes as if trying to decide whether he was being serious. Then, they started to cry and ran back to their parents.

"Not cool, dude," Dave said.

"Yeah. A little unnecessary," Maria agreed.

Henk didn't care. Even when the parents shook their heads and shot him daggers. And why should he? Sorrow's history was not something to be turned into a sideshow attraction that made a mockery of all those that have lost their lives, and he certainly was not okay with being a poster boy for the place.

In the daylight, he could see that the town was a vastly different place than it used to be. Colourful signposts were at every street corner, marking the way to famous murder sites, and he was pretty sure he could see a guy walking around in a giant fuzzy mascot suit that had been made to look like the Yellow Hammer (a burly humanoid with hammers for hands and feet). It was. The Yellow Hammer mascot stopped to pose for pictures with kids, pretending to smash them with his giant foam hammer-hands.

"Do you guys seriously not see anything wrong with this?" Henk asked as they passed a hot food stand selling 'finger' hot dogs and 'special' meat burgers.

"I think it's awesome," Dave said. "If I knew Sorrow was going to turn out like this, I'm not sure I would have left."

"I think it's fun," Maria smiled. "Harman's meat business is booming, and I get to make lots of kids happy."

They stepped aside to avoid a group of children running along the pavement. Each wore a fluorescent vest and had a matching backpack with their school's crest. The teacher mumbled an apology as she hurried after them. Henk watched as they joined the back of a long queue that led inside the town morgue. A large sign was embedded in the grass out front: SUICIDE SITE 17.

Henk couldn't believe what he was seeing. He stormed across the road and pushed through the adults and children waiting to get a peek inside. Several people whispered his name while others yelled it outright, asking for photos and autographs. Henk ignored them all and pushed through the open doors. A barrier belt blocked his approach as the queue wound round to the left, but he snapped the belt free from the stand and continued ahead on the most direct route.

There were two metal beds inside the autopsy room (obscured by plexiglass to ensure visitors could not pass a certain point). Each bed had a pile of folded clothes at one end on which a featureless mannequin rested its head. The mannequin's throats had been painted with excruciating attention to detail to appear as if they had been severed entirely. More red paint was dotted around the floor beneath their dangling arms. On the far wall, beyond the autopsy tables, an unseen projector displayed a black and white crime scene photo of his parents with the words 'The Wolfe Suicide Pact.' Their faces had been blurred, at least, but it did little to lessen the bile rising at the back of Henk's throat. He took one look at the smiling faces of the children all around him, then projectile vomited against the plexiglass wall, spraying the kids standing either side of him.

Screams, shouts, and angry words filled the narrow space, but Henk had his own thoughts he wanted to get across. He began shouting obscenities at the crowd around him, rancid spittle spraying from his wet lips as he shamed them for finding entertainment in his parents' deaths.

Maria and Dave watched on in stunned silence.

Chapter 8

Case Two: The Goblin. May 8th, 2008

Henk placed a hand in the middle of the small table his dad had pulleyed up to the treehouse. Dave and Maria put their hands on top of his. "Sons of Sorrow 'till the end," he said.

"Sons of Sorrow," they responded.

"I still don't know why we have to be called the *Sons* of Sorrow," Maria pouted. "I'm a girl."

"Sons and Sisters of Sorrow doesn't sound as cool," Dave said as he exited the wooden shack and tossed his backpack down to the ground.

"It's not Sons in the literal sense of the word," Henk agreed. "Think of it as a metaphor."

Back down at ground level, Maria said, "Sisters of Sorrow could be a metaphor." The brothers simply looked at her. "Just saying."

The Goblin had been spotted in and around Sorrow Cemetery for several weeks. The squat figure's intentions were unclear, but unlikely to be anything good given its appearance and the location it was frequenting. It was the Sons of Sorrow's second 'case'. They were not getting paid for their services, nor were they recognised as a crimefighting trio in any official capacity. Still, following their victory over the Wailing Widow, they'd decided they could do a better job of keeping the town safe than the slothful brothers that passed as the law in their county.

The Bendersons were more interested in watching trash TV and gambling away their paltry wages than protecting what they would openly call their 'lost cause' of a community. Bobby Benderson was short, fat, and every bit as stereotypical as you may expect. He wore his blonde hair in large spikes to give him more height and would try all manner of stretches and postures to appear larger (when what he should really have been worried about was his weight). Billy Benderson was the polar opposite— tall, bald, and hunched. Bobby and Billy would never have overseen Sorrow's law department had their father not been on the council at the time the previous officers were cut into cubes by the Square Boi Slasher, a schizophrenic math teacher that had only been caught after he started writing equations on the board in the blood of his victims during class (it was later established that the man had been possessed by a demonic calculator he'd found while walking in the woods).

Brett Benderson was in Henk's history class and was just as much of an incompetent waste of space as his parents. It was unclear whether Brett was the son of Bobby or Billy, as the brothers were both having unprotected sex with the same woman. A woman that seriously needed to reconsider her life choices.

It was a little after midnight, and a thin fog had begun to settle across the ground, obscuring the curling smile of the half-moon and giving the woods an otherworldly quality.

"What do you think the Goblin is?" Dave asked, despite their agreement to keep quiet less than a minute prior. "If you're right, I'll pay you back that tenner."

Henk smacked him on the shoulder. "You'll pay me back anyway. You owe me."

"My guess is Bobby Benderson," Maria whispered. "Similar height, similar build."

"The cop?" Dave said as if it was an awful guess. "No way that fat bastard would be out and about this time of night. It's rare enough to see him outside the station."

"It was a good a guess as any," Henk said in Maria's defence. "But I'd be surprised if it was Bobby Benderson."

"All right, so who do *you* think it is?"

Henk pretended to think on it for a moment, then said, "I don't think it's a person at all."

The others rolled their eyes collectively. Dave said, "Come on, man. Goblins don't exist."

"If you'd told me the Spectre and the Shades were real a few months back, I would have said the same thing. If ghosts are real, why can't goblins be?"

"We should probably deal with those guys soon," Dave said. "But getting back to the point, goblins were invented for fairytales. Ask anyone, and they'll tell you as much. Ghosts, on the other hand, are far more common."

Maria pouted and looked at Henk with a glint in her eye. "Aw. Let little Henkie believe in whatever he wants. Next, you'll be telling him Santa doesn't exist."

"Fine," Henk said. "I'll take the bet."

They continued through the woods for several minutes, making sure to stay off the main paths so as not to give themselves away. A spreading ground fog made progress slower than they would have liked, but they managed to avoid getting turned around and eventually reached a clearing. Sorrow cemetery had two entrances and a low metal fence around the perimeter, which could be disconnected and expanded when required, which was handy, as it was required often. The gang split up at the treeline and made their way to their positions. Maria hid near the nearest set of gates, Dave took the far entrance, and Henk continued round to the opposite side of the cemetery, slipping behind a towering elm. Settled into their positions, they bedded in for what could potentially be a long night.

Within moments there was noise from the direction of the main footpath. Thanks to the fog, it was hard to be sure, but it appeared to be the Goblin. The hunched figure moved slowly

71

toward the centre of the graveyard, stopping in front of a large, cracked tombstone. It then reached a clawed hand into the opposite sleeve of its hooded robe and produced a curved blade, which it used to take scrapings from the face of the grave marker. The Goblin then moved to the next tombstone and repeated the process, and again, with a third. Henk adjusted his position as it then spat on the fistful of collected grave dust, got to its knees. Its hand disappeared into its robes, and its body began to jerk violently. After a minute or so, the gnarled hand reappeared, gravestone dust and phlegm now smeared all over it, and it started digging a small hole in the earth over one of the fresher graves.

Closest to the Goblin, Henk could tell that the grave it was clawing at belonged to that of Rhia Fredericks, an attractive girl a few years his senior that had hung herself from Bellwater Bridge a few months prior. He moved to leave his cover. The creature stopped digging. It checked its surroundings, then hitched the cloak up to its waist. Henk cringed as a pathetic penis sprung up, the narrow helmet glistening in the moonlight and the shaft lathered in a suit of grave dust. The Goblin stroked itself a couple of times before lying flat on the ground and starting to pump away at the loose soil.

"Stay where you are," Dave said, pointing a can of pepper spray at the demon's direction.

"Don't move, pervert" Maria added, polished knuckledusters on either fist.

Whatever it was appeared to understand English, as it immediately stopped humping the grave and hitched its trousers back up. It sat there on its haunches, looking from Dave to Maria as if it were about to take flight.

Henk was ready for it when it made its move. Failing to check behind it, the Goblin took Henk's fist to the chin, cracking its head on Rhia's gravestone on its way to the floor. It lay unmoving, its neck bent awkwardly against the granite.

Dave slid the pepper spray back into his bag. "That was easy. I was hoping it would have put up a bit more of a fight."

"Still confident it's a real goblin?" Maria teased.

After what they'd just witnessed, Henk wasn't sure about anything. But that didn't mean he wouldn't be stubborn until the end. "Sure," he said. "Why not."

Dave rubbed his hands together gleefully. "All right then. Let's see who this Goblin really is."

Henk took the Goblin's ankles (which appeared human) and dragged it away from the grave marker. He rolled the figure onto its back and grabbed a fistful of the oversized hood. A brief pause for dramatic effect, then—

"No fucking way!" Dave doubled over, laughter quickly turning into wheezing as he tripped and smashed his teeth against a grave.

Ignoring him, Maria folded her arms across her chest and cocked her head to the side, appraising the Goblin. "Do you think he's okay? He's bleeding pretty bad."

Henk agreed with her observation, crouched beside Brett Benderson and put a finger to the side of his throat. It wouldn't be the end of the world if the rapey motherfucker were dead, but given his parents were 'police', it would make things easier if he weren't. There was a faint pulse. "He's fine."

Dave had finally pulled himself together enough to string together a sentence, "You nearly killed the cop's son!"

"I was just doing what we came here to do."

Maria joined Henk at the Goblin's side to get a closer look at the weeping wound above his right eyebrow. "What do we do with him now? I can't imagine the Bendersons will take too kindly to us knocking out their kid."

"We leave him here," Henk said, standing up. He helped Maria back to her feet and caught a delicious taste of her watermelon body spray. "He knows he's been caught, and he knows who caught him. I don't think he'll be doing . . . whatever the fuck this was . . . ever again."

"I hope you're right," Maria said. "It would be so easy to cut his fucking throat right now."

Henk looked at Dave, who looked at Maria. It was one of those times that she managed to shock them both. Usually happy-go-lucky, it would be easy for someone who had just met her to believe she were a pushover, a princess away with the fairies. But Maria had another side that only showed itself on infrequent occasions.

"Yeah," Dave muttered. "Or, we could leave him to think about what he's done. I think Henk's right. Brett hasn't technically hurt anyone other than himself. And any plans I had for my own funeral. After seeing this, I want to be cremated and scattered the fuck away from here."

Maria giggled. Back to her usual self.

74

They stood over Brett's unconscious body, linked hands, and shouted, "SONS OF SORROW."

Chapter 9

Henk was feeling a little better after a 'special' burger and a bottle of water. That's not to say he was okay with what he'd just seen, but at least he didn't feel sick anymore.

"I'm sorry, I probably should have warned you about that," Maria said as they resumed the trek to the church. "I'm such a CUNT." Parents pulled their kids out of the way, scowling at her. She slumped her shoulders, coughed delicately onto the back of her hand. "I don't deserve to get married. All I ever think about is myself."

"And you have every right to," Henk said.

Dave was about to spark up a fat joint of mo-gro when a wiry figure in a blue uniform broke away from a group of concerned parents to block their path. The policeman slapped his baton into his open palm. "Well, well, well. Guess some things never change. Bet you thought we'd seen the last of these losers, hey, Maria?"

"I invited them, actually," Maria said, linking her arm through Henk's. "And they've been nothing but helpful to me since they've been back."

"Knob Goblin?" Dave gawked. "Is that really you?"

Henk approached the officer and swept the blonde fringe away from his forehead to reveal a large scar. "Huh. It is him. Didn't realise they allowed necrophiliacs on the force."

75

Brett Benderson scowled and immediately looked around to ensure the rest of the community was not within earshot. He offered a forced smile and a nod to the parents that had sent him over. "I never had sex with . . ." he slid the baton into the holster on his belt. "You know what? Forget it. Why are you here? And Dave? Put that baggie away. You can't smoke weed around here. I'll have to arrest you."

"Try it," Dave said, shoving the blue buds back into his pocket like a sulking teen regardless. "Besides, it's mo-gro, which I think you'll find isn't recognised by the law."

Brett pursed his lips, narrowed his eyes, then backed down. As everyone knew he would. No matter how hard he tried to assert his dominance, he was in debt to them for the rest of his life. They'd stolen his robes to prove to the rest of the town that the Goblin was no more but had ultimately decided against unveiling his identity.

"We're looking for Maria's fiancée," Henk said. "Have you seen him?"

Brett's thick brow sunk to the bridge of his nose—he looked as if he was already done with the conversation and wanted to get away from the reminder of his dark past as soon as possible. Finally, he grumbled, "If you've got a missing persons case, you should have contacted the police."

"Thanks, but we're doing just fine without you and your dad," Maria said.

"Dad?" Dave said, "You found out which one of those inbreds knocked up your mum?"

"Bobby died five years ago. Massive heart attack. Billy is my dad."

Maria repeated, "Have you seen Harman?"

"No. As a matter of fact, I'm investigating several missing persons reports at this moment. Tell me, Henk, Dave, when did you arrive back in town?"

"Piss off limp dick," Dave said. "This is serious. We might be dealing with a case for the Sons of Sorrow." Henk cringed. Dave continued as if he hadn't noticed: "Harman's disappearance may be related. Or maybe not. If you don't know anything, then get out of our way because we've got a job to do."

"As do I. We've not had any trouble here for a long time, boys. It strikes me as a little strange how the 'Sons of Sorrow' return at the same time as people start disappearing, and I think we know how you guys like to 'handle' your 'cases'."

"What are you talking about? No trouble?" Henk said. "We know all about the fingers. And can you stop doing air quotes? You look like a total dick."

"Yes, well."

A young girl with black pigtails ran up to Officer Benderson. She wore an oversized jumper with a cartoon picture of the Head on the front and was screaming about losing her parents.

"I'll be watching you," Brett said as the others walked away.

"What a limp dick," Dave muttered as soon as his back was turned. "Some things never change indeed."

St Augustine's church was located at the end of a row of residential houses on the west side of the village, an area with only minor macabre occurrences (within recent decades), therefore removed from the bustle of tourism. It was cooler, quieter, and Henk felt himself beginning to relax a little now that he was away from the crowd of starstruck strangers. He had no idea how Maria could put up with it every day, but he supposed not everyone hated people as much as he did. The building itself towered over the surrounding cottages, with intricate stained-glass windows on all sides and a large bell tower that had stood empty for as long as any of them had been alive. The façade had been designed with near-perfect symmetry.

Dave polished off his joint and flicked the butt into someone's front garden without a second thought. As Maria tutted and went to retrieve it, Henk couldn't help but notice he could see straight through the house and into the back garden. It was completely barren. The next house was the same, as was the one after that.

"It's still weird seeing so much of the place deserted," he said, mainly to himself.

Maria dropped the roach down a nearby drain. "Most people left before we became well-known. Lots of people were killing themselves. I guess they thought it was contagious or something. When the council made a last-ditch effort to try and bring some business back to the town, it drove away even more of the people that lived here."

"People don't want to be reminded of the awful things that have happened around them," Dave said.

"That, and it became *too* popular. I don't mind, myself, but I know many others saw the pace of life as one of Sorrow's redeeming features. These days, you can't walk through town without someone asking you for directions or a camera being pointed in your face."

Once again, Henk reasserted he'd made the right decision in leaving when he did. There had been nothing left for him in Sorrow, and if he'd had to deal with what Maria was describing every day of his life, he *definitely* would have topped himself.

"The plus side is there are plenty of places for sale in Sorrow," Maria poked Henk in the ribs playfully and offered a smile that reached her ears. "The tourists like to visit, but they never stay for longer than a few days. They don't appreciate the place the way a true Sorrownian does."

"Yarr," Dave said with a ridiculous pirate accent. "Sorrow runs through me veins."

"More like they're happy to visit because they know that have a safe home miles away once they're done taking in the grizzly sights and stories," Henk said.

The church doors stood open, offering a view of a stunning technicolour interior as the mid-morning light shone through the stained glass. It was almost enough to make one forget where they were. But not quite. Maria led the way up the short flight of steps with Henk and Dave close behind.

The only time the brothers had ever set foot in St Augustine's was on the day of their parent's funeral. It was a quiet affair with a short, concise service. As the older of the two kids, Henk had intended to say a few words to the meagre audience, but he'd passed out, perhaps mercifully, and had only awoken after the service was finished. It was likely because of this that returning to the majestic building was not too much of an issue for him—he could hardly remember the day.

"Pastor Wicker?" Maria called. Her voice echoed around the high-ceilinged chamber.

They walked up the central aisle, through row upon row of polished mahogany benches, to the altar on the raised platform at the far end. Dave looked up to the vaulted roof with a sense of wonder, his mouth open like a virgin who'd just stumbled into an orgy. "It's mad if you really think about it," he said." "Like, how they built this place. I wouldn't even know where to start."

Henk stared at him. "That's because you're not an architect."

"They didn't have architects back then! They did it with no cranes on anything, either. Aliens, man. I'm telling you. It's been proven that they helped build the pyramids, so this would be a piece of cake."

Henk narrowed his eyes as he considered how to reply but was saved from Dave's monologue by the sound of Maria knocking on an arched wooden door in the far-left corner next to a concrete statue of the Virgin Mary. "Pastor?" She looked over her shoulder and motioned for Henk to follow.

"Should we be going in there?" Henk said.

"It's fine. I've been back here plenty of times."

The door opened onto a narrow hallway, which, from the outside of the building, should not have been there at all. A light came from beneath another door at the far end. There was a faint thumping noise and a series of strained groans. Maria ran for the door while Henk and Dave hung back a little, wary of what they may find the Pastor doing on the other side.

"Oh, god. Help me!" Maria cried.

It was a storage room of sorts. Pastor Wicker was suspended from the ceiling by a length of rubber tubing around his neck. His face was bright red, his eyes wide, and the spotlights shone off his bald dome. Henk ran to the holy man and wrapped his arms around his kicking legs while Maria picked up the wooden chair that he'd leapt from and put it back under his feet. He resisted at first, uttering a gurgled curse as he tried to keep his legs away from the support, but Henk held him firm and together, they managed to force him to stand. A moment later, Dave, who had been busy with his own plan of attack, leapt from a second chair and wrapped both hands around the length of rubber tubing, intending to tear it free of the ceiling. His aim was true, and he brought both the ceiling fan and a section of plasterboard. Dave landed on his back, the tubing still clasped in his hands, while plaster and wood rained down on the lot of them. "The fuck kind of terminator rubber is this?" he groaned.

Henk had managed to keep the Pastor upright during the ordeal, and with the extra slack, was able to lower him to the floor for Maria to go about untying the slipknot around his neck. After a nerve-wracking moment, she was able to get her nails into the resilient material and prise the knot apart. Pastor Clive Wicker immediately began to cough, a spray of gunky blood splattering across the concrete floor from his chewed cheeks.

"Get him some water," Maria said to Dave.

He shuffled out of the room, holding his back, and returned a minute later with a goblet of what was most likely holy water. Pastor Wicker took it in both hands and tipped it to his mouth. After swilling it around a few times, he spat it out onto the floor, then repeated the process until the water turned a little clearer. The others stood around awkwardly, waiting for the suicidal man to say something.

Finally, Dave broke the tension. "You're welcome."

The Pastor placed the goblet on the floor next to the puddle of bloody water and looked at Dave over the top of his wire-rimmed glasses. "You should have let me die. I wanted to die."

No one bothered to ask him *why* he wanted to die. In Sorrow, sometimes you just did. "Wouldn't you be condemning yourself to hell by committing suicide?" Henk asked. He extended a hand to the Pastor, but Wicker knocked it aside and pulled himself to his feet with a scowl on his face. With not an inch of fat on him, he looked like an angry skeleton.

"Look around you," he said, "We're living in hell."

Dave's stoned eyes widened. He looked around the room as if he expected a demon to jump out of anything. Several fingers sprouted on the ends of his own, and an elbow appeared to be forming in place of his nose.

"Come on, Wicker," Henk said. "You know as well as any of us that Sorrow has always been like this. Why now?"

"You should never have come back."

"Why does everyone keep saying that?" Dave said.

"It won't let you go again." Wicker looked to Henk, "You feel it, don't you?"

The two shared a silent understanding. The truth was, Henk *could* feel it. Whatever 'it' was. Was the Pastor talking about the ever-present feeling of dread? Or something else? "Tell me what you know."

Pastor Wicker adjusted his clerical collar. His face was regaining some of its natural colour. "I have been unfaithful to the Lord, and I cannot protect the town from the evils that are coming. My prayers are no longer enough."

"Pretty selfish of you to try and kill yourself when you're supposed to be officiating a wedding in a few days," Maria said, trying to bring the conversation round to the reason they were there in the first place.

Wicker shouldered past her and started down the corridor. He muttered over his shoulder, "Something tells me you're not here about the wedding. Jeff still alive?"

"Why would you ask that?"

The older man ignored her as he continued through the door at the other end, the others hot on his tail. He reached the altar and stopped, turned to face them.

"Where is he?" Maria demanded. Henk and Dave stood ready to tackle the Pastor should he try and flee.

"I have to show you something," Wicker said, ignoring the question once again. He approached the pipe organ at the back of the raised platform and lifted the cover.

"Quit fucking around and answer the lady," Dave said.

Pastor Wicker kept his back to them as he banged out a series of off-pitch notes. Henk was expecting something extraordinary to happen, like the floor to open up or the pipe organ to slide back into the wall. Instead, a small aperture on the side of the wooden podium popped to the side to reveal a brass key. Wicker retrieved it, then re-entered the corridor they'd just come out of. Frustration growing, Henk followed. Wicker stopped halfway up the hallway and slid the key into a small hole in the wall. He then pushed open a thin door and entered without looking back.

The door led onto rocky ground, which descended sharply before eventually levelling out. The Pastor strolled ahead confidently, as if he'd been down there a hundred times and knew the footing without looking. The air was musky, and Henk found himself thankful that he did not suffer from claustrophobia. Regardless, he followed without hesitation, his curiosity overpowering all else. The bald man knew something they didn't. Something important.

The walls dampened the further they progressed, the only sound that of their scuffing footsteps and anxious breaths. Eventually, after what felt like at least an hour (but in reality, was a few minutes), the path opened into a large chamber. Henk froze. Maria walked into him.

The walls were plastered in the bioluminescent fingers. The glow they gave off was enough to light the large chamber without the need for torches. Henk stowed his phone slowly without taking his eyes off the Pastor. Was he working with the Head? Had they walked straight into a trap?

"Don't worry," Wicker said. He motioned for Henk and the others to enter and ran a hand along one of the luminous appendages to show it was safe. "They're perfectly harmless."

"What *is* this place?" Dave gawked.

Maria remained silent. It was hard to tell if she was taken aback by what they were seeing or if she was simply beyond the point of caring. For all the strange shit that had been going on, they were still no closer to finding her fiancé.

There was a large shrine in the middle of the room. Wicker approached it and lit several of the small candles dotted around it. At the top was a three-sided wooden crate, with a plush red pillow on the base and back.

"The Head is turning against us," the Pastor said calmly. He bent to pick up one of the candles and moved it closer to the crate, illuminating a cracked, leatherbound book. "We thought we were doing the right thing, for the town, and for the Head."

"What are you talking about?" Henk asked. He pointed to the book, "And what's that?"

Wicker flicked through the pages until he landed on the one he was looking for, then turned the book and displayed the yellowed paper to the others.

The Head stared back at them, along with a dozen or so depictions of smaller creatures and illegible scribblings.

"The Head," Wicker said, snapping the book shut with a loud clap that ricocheted around the chamber. "It is unclear when, exactly, it was initially discovered, but we suspect the first settlers of Sorrow stumbled upon it and failed to treat it with respect. This led to their subsequent insanity and suicide."

"Slow down," Henk said. "What did you mean by 'doing the right thing for the town'?"

"Please," Wicker said. "Give me a moment to explain. You see, the Head feeds on sadness. Those with a negative outlook are more prone to its call, if you will, and can be driven to suicide if they're not careful."

"It eats people?!" Dave said, looking warily at the digits.

"It eats *sadness*," the Pastor said, wagging a thin finger. "Well, mostly. For decades, the council been able to keep it docile by purposefully altering the ambient energy in the village. Certain members of our community volunteered to make themselves sad, depressed, or just a little miserable. But some would reach a certain point only to find they could not return. Many good people have died protecting this town and those that they love."

Henk cleared his throat, surprised to find it incredibly dry. "You're not about to tell me our parents . . ."

Wicker nodded gravely. "Your parents paid the ultimate price for the safety of Sorrow, and their sacrifice will never be forgotten."

Henk felt as if he'd been hit in the chest by a brick. On the one hand, he finally had a reason for the way things played out the way they did, but on the other, he was angry. How could they have volunteered for such a thing, knowing the risks? Why didn't they just move away from Sorrow?

Enjoying the story, Dave said, "Far out, man."

The Pastor continued: "Over the years, we lost several more. Some became afraid that the Head was growing too strong and moved away, leaving the rest of us to deal with it. As I'm sure you're aware, there are only a handful of townsfolk left, which is why we decided to start bringing in tourists. You're never too far from a crying child or a lover's quarrel, but it still wasn't enough. It needed more. The council agreed that drastic measures had to be taken to secure the town's future. You must understand we were only doing what we believed was best. To keep the residents and visitors safe." He paused, cast a withered hand about the chamber, "The fingers started appearing soon after."

"So, we kill it," Dave said. "How hard can it be?"

"EVERYONE SHUTTHEFUCKUP." Maria's shriek echoed for several seconds before finally escaping through the cracks in the rock walls. "Wicker. Jeff was taken by these things earlier this morning. Harman is missing. I need you to tell us something that can help me."

"I'm sorry, Miss Wendall, but I'm afraid he may already be gone."

"Gone?"

Dave rounded on the Pastor. "Just tell us what we want to know, and we'll get out of here."

Wicker placed the tome gently back on the altar. "The Head seems to bring others from their world to ours, whether it means to or not. The strange entities that appear from time to time . . . it's all connected. If only we knew what it wanted, we might be able to appease it once and for all."

"The rift," Dave said. "I thought we closed that."

Wicker was becoming visibly agitated, his eyes flicking between the three. "There is nothing you can do. There is no escape!"

"Where," Dave growled, looking as if he was about to attack. "Where is it now?"

"Dave," Henk said gently. "Don't."

Dave didn't get a chance to do anything.

Pastor Wicker had been silently peeling the metal casing from the tealight clutched in his hands. He brought it up to his throat and gouged a sizeable trench without warning.

"NO!" Henk cried as the Pastor dropped to his knees, the wound rapidly filling and overflowing with blood. "Help me!"

Maria leapt to action, pressing both hands to the holy man's throat. Wicker fell backwards, landing on the shrine and knocking several candles flying. Henk kicked them away to stop the flames from catching their clothing. Dave seemed unable to move, shocked by the sudden turn of events. "Guys," he mumbled.

"Dave," Henk said without looking back. "Give me your shirt!"

"Guys, we need to get out of here." They were too busy trying to keep Wicker alive to pay any attention to Dave's plea. "GUYS!"

Henk fell sidewards when he saw what the problem was.

The fingers were slithering down the walls, crisscrossing over one another as they raced to be the first one to reach the Pastor. Henk grabbed Maria by the wrist and pulled her back as the first of the bioluminescent fingers reached the dying man and wrapped itself around his throat. It pulsed violently, appeared to be syphoning the man's blood.

"Wait!" Maria screamed. She pulled away from Henk and dived for the book as a second vine-like finger reached Wicker, wrapped itself around his arm. Then, a third, this one around his chest. Within seconds, Pastor Wicker was hidden beneath a blanket of writhing, tentacle-like fingers, his flesh bubbling beneath their touch.

Chapter 10

"Cup of tea?" Henk asked from the kitchen doorway. Maria shook her head, running her fingertips up and down her things. Dave asked if she had any beer, to which she nodded. Henk returned with a cold beer for Dave and another for himself a moment later.

It was late, and Maria had asked the others if they would stay with her as she didn't want to be alone. The atmosphere in the living room was tense and a little awkward, mentally exhausted both from what had happened to Wicker and from a day of fruitless searching for Harman.

"We should make an official report with the police," Henk suggested. As much as he hated the Knob Goblin, it seemed like the right time to admit defeat.

Maria sniffled. She took Henk's beer and drained a quarter of it in one go. "They aren't going to be any help. Brett and Billy couldn't find a whore in a brothel." Dave snorted, then stopped as he remembered the seriousness of the situation. "Besides, Brett already knows Harman is missing, and it sounds like he's not the only one."

"Well, what about that?" Henk nodded to the thick tome on the coffee table. None of them had wanted to touch it since arriving back. The leathery cover was blank, burnt in patches, and covered in dark brown stains.

"What about it?" Dave said. "Do *you* want to touch it?"

Maria leant forward and snatched it with both hands. "It's all written in gibberish," she said as she began flicking through the pages. "I'm not sure this is going to be much help to us either."

"Woah, wait a minute," Henk said. "Go back." He shuffled closer, slammed a finger on the open page. "There. Look at that and tell me it's not what I think it is."

Dave got up from his chair and came around the back of the sofa to peek over Henk's shoulder. "That's weird. What did he say this book was?"

"He didn't."

The three of them were silent for a minute, studying the line drawing of the Gloved King. The dimensions were slightly off, but there was no denying the crude sketch was that of the entity that had terrorised the village. Henk motioned for Maria to keep going.

More of the same. For every being they'd defeated over the years, there were at least a dozen they'd never encountered, interspersed with pages crammed with illegible writing. The last half of the book was devoted entirely to the Head, although whatever its 'real' name was, was still up for debate. There was plenty of text to accompany the drawings, but none of it made any sense. Only one thing was certain in their minds. Everything wrong with Sorrow could be traced back to it.

"It's useless," Maria said, shoving the book from her lap to the floor. "So, these things exist because of the rift, which exists because of the Head. Or is it the Head that exists because of the rift? How does that help us right now?"

"We'll figure it out," Henk said gently. It was frustrating to know the answers to every question they had were likely staring them in the face, if only they could understand the text. He slumped back and put an arm around Maria without thinking.

"There's still one avenue we haven't exhausted," Dave said. Henk looked up from his empty beer half-heartedly. "The Gimp."

"This is no time for stupid jokes, Dave. You know, maybe everyone was right. Maybe we shouldn't have come back."

"The Gimp is in the book, too," Dave said. He placed his beer on the coffee table and picked the book up from where it had landed. "See?"

Henk perked up. "Maria?"

She lifted her head from his shoulder.

"Do you know who that actually is, inside the gimp suit?"

"I used to think it was Wicker, but after seeing him today, I'm not so sure."

"Wicker's slightly taller," Dave agreed. "Can you think of anyone else?"

Maria shook her head. Her cheeks were rosy, her eyes wet. Henk couldn't help but think how cute she looked at that moment, despite how inappropriate it was given the circumstances.

"Well, I'm gonna hit the sack," Dave said. "We should head back out early. Don't worry, Maria. There's still plenty of time for Harman to show."

They wished Dave goodnight then sat in silence until they heard the door to the spare bedroom close. Henk wanted to offer words of reassurance, but he found he could not share Dave's optimism. In truth, he could tell the Pastor's death had shaken Dave, not that he would ever show it. He couldn't blame him, either. They'd seen a lot of death between them but that . . . that was something else. The entire situation was starting to get to him.

Maria returned from the fireplace, having added another log while Henk was lost in thought. To his surprise, she took a seat right up against him on the sofa and snuggled into his chest. Her hair smelled incredible, yet he fought the urge to kiss the top of her head.

"Can I tell you something?" Maria said. Her hand rose from her lap and started stroking Henk's chest.

"S-sure," he said. He was familiar with Maria's habit of stroking things when stressed and found himself suddenly terrified he would get an erection. Or maybe he should . . . no, *inappropriate!*

"When we were younger, I always kinda liked you."

"I liked you too, Maria. I still do."

"No, I mean *liked* you liked you. Before Harman, of course."

A cascade of unwelcome thoughts rained down on him. The hours wasted daydreaming about how different his life could have been. All he could say was, "Oh."

"I thought you liked me, too. But you never said anything. I mean, I even gave you a handy after your parents died, and you didn't get the hint."

"I thought you were just stressed."

"And then you said you were leaving . . ." Maria's hand froze as if she had just realised what it was doing. "I don't know," she mumbled. "I thought we could have been something."

"But . . . you were with Harman?" he croaked. "I . . . he was with you at your house."

"His dad came to see my stepdad. You remember they used to play poker together every Friday? Well, Jeff had come to pay his losses. Harman came along with him."

Henk shifted uncomfortably, his inner voice telling him he was an even bigger loser than he'd thought. His own inability to ask her to be with him had pushed her straight into the arms of another man (or boy, as it was then). "Oh."

Maria sat up suddenly, leaving Henk dying for more. It was all his fault. She looked him dead in the eyes. "You hurt me, Henk. You guys were all I had back then. But you left. You never called; you never wrote. It was as if I just ceased to exist in your world."

Henk wanted to tell her she couldn't be further from the truth. He wanted to tell her he'd tried to call, but under the impression she'd been dating someone else, he would never know what to say. He wanted to write her letters, but even writing the town's name brought back too many memories and sent him spiralling off the edge of sanity into depression for weeks on end. The only thing he could do for a long time was simply pretend that the town and the things that happened were nothing but a series of bad dreams. He wanted to tell her that not a day passed that he didn't think of her, wonder what she was doing.

But now, she was standing up, and his mouth refused to coordinate with his brain. Even now, refused to say the things that he wanted to. Right then, he understood that Maria was his kryptonite. She always was, always would be, and whether he thought he was not good enough for her or simply too afraid of fucking things up, he could never tell her what he wished he could. Not that it even mattered anymore—that ship had sailed so long ago it had hit an iceberg and was now resting on the seabed.

"I just thought you should know," she said, gathering the empty beer bottles, now unwilling to make eye contact. "But I still appreciate you being here now."

With that, she left, returning only momentarily to pass him a blanket for the night on the couch. He lay there for several hours, unable to sleep, his mind whirling faster than it had done for many years.

Was it really a set of unfortunate circumstances, or had the Head had a hand in everything, right from the start? If it was as old as Wicker claimed, not only was it responsible for their parents' deaths, Dave's, and countless others, but it was also responsible for the deaths and suffering caused by the rest of the entities over the years. Entities that the Sons of Sorrow put back in the dirt.

Except for the Gimp. If the Gimp had been causing harm to the villagers, Henk had no doubt that something would have been done about it a long time ago, but he'd seen it with his own eyes, and although a little strange, it did not appear to pose any threat. Whoever was inside the liquid latex seemed more shocked to see them than they were him. Hell—he'd even seen a *Sightings of the Gimp!* stand in the town square, for visitors to post their own photos of the Gimp. That could be part of the issue, Henk reasoned. Sorrow had become too commercialised. Fucked-up things could be happening all around, and people and they would think it was just part of the show. Things might have been no better than they used to be. Only people didn't realise it. A mysterious figure snatching someone away with a bloodied sword could be something to bring applause, all part of the show. With so few original inhabitants left, who would know fact from fiction? Even the people working the attractions were out-of-towners.

Henk eventually drifted off a little after four in the morning. He did not dream.

He remembered.

Chapter 11

Case Three: The Shapeshifter. July 17th, 2008

The Sons of Sorrow were still coasting off the success of their second victory when they got wind of another case. Three students from their college had gone missing over two weeks. First, Alice Yale, a blonde-haired, blue-eyed supermodel in the making. Next was Francie Byerly, Alice's best friend and another walking icon of lust among classmates and teachers alike. By the time Jenni Grant vanished from her bedroom in the dead of night without a trace, it had become as clear as a slap to the face that they were dealing with something unnatural.

One advantage of living in a relatively small community was people tended to notice when something is different. An extra treadmill appeared in Jimmy's Gym, the same make and model as the others—no one could say where it came from, yet it was gone again the following morning. Builders working on the roof of St Augustine's were questioning where a second portaloo had come from—identical to the one standing next to it down to the loose door hinge and the deep scratch in the plastic above the toilet seat. This, too, was gone the next day without a trace or explanation. It was only when Henk and Dave witnessed a telephone box up and run away that they concluded they must be dealing with a shapeshifter. Their experience with dealing with such a thing was non-existent, so after meeting up with Maria, they formulated a plan using the limited information they had to go by.

Something was roaming the streets that could imitate the appearance of things around it. Something with a taste for college girls. Knowing the missing girls were likely already dead, a rescue mission was out of the question. They had to find a way of stopping the creature before it could attack again, and with no better option presenting itself . . .

"I'm not so sure about this, guys," Maria whispered into the walkie talkie clipped to the lapel of her coat. It was a little after midnight, and she was dressed in a short skirt despite the chill in the air. Henk and Dave remained at a safe distance further up the road in the thick shadow of a shop awning, where they could keep Maria in sight while not being obvious to anyone (or anything) else as she paced the quiet road.

The town was silent. Maria's footsteps resonated off the store fronts. Somewhere in the distance, an owl screeched, causing her to flinch.

"MARIA CLEMENECE WENDALL."

Maria spun on her heel, reflexes on high alert.

"What are you doing out here alone at this hour? Your father and I have been so worried about you, what with all these missing girls recently. We were minutes from calling the police."

"I-I was just taking a walk. I felt a little woozy and wanted some fresh air."

Maria's mother placed her hands on her shapely hips. Dark crescent moons hung from her lower eyelids. She looked as if she didn't believe a single word her daughter was saying but was too tired to argue. Instead, she rolled her eyes. "The car is down the road. If we get home quick, we might be able to prevent your father from rallying a mob."

Maria looked over her shoulder, mouthed what appeared to be *sorry* to the others, and hurried after her mother in the opposite direction.

Dave stepped out from their cover. "Well, guess I'm going to head back, too. Not much point hanging around without any bait. Try again tomorrow?"

Henk laughed. "Depends if Maria's parents have killed her by then."

"Good point. Catch you at the orphanage, man."

Henk started in the direction Maria had left moments before, while Dave went the opposite. He pulled his jacket closer to his neck against the biting chill, then buried his fists in his pockets, gripping the object tight in his right hand. Ahead and to his left was a wide alleyway that ran between the barbers and a laundrette, through to Edward Street running parallel. Dampened voices travelled on the wind, and after checking around him, Henk hurried down the alley. "Hey, is that you, Maria?"

"Henk? What are you doing here?" she replied, doing her best to sound surprised.

Maria's mother remained silent, her face undiscernible within a dark blob of shadow.

"I was just out for a run. Thought I heard your voice. Did you drive here, Mrs Wendall? Mind if I catch a ride home?"

Mrs Wendall swayed gently from side to side. Maria took a slow step away from her. "Mum?"

The thing that was presenting as Maria's mother screeched as Dave leapt on her from behind, burying a kitchen knife in her neck. Maria immediately followed up with a wide sweep, planting her blade in her 'mother's' nasal cavity. Henk jumped in as the shapeshifter threw an elbow, catching Dave in the face and sending him reeling to the floor, and plunged his knife into her stomach with a wet sucking sound.

The shapeshifter uttered a guttural growl as it melted to a black, sludgy puddle before their eyes and began to slink away from them. Their weapons clattered to the floor as the thing continued its retreat. "Shit!" Dave yelled, "What now?" The being had disappeared out the end of the alley. They chased it across the road and around the back of a corner shop.

It was gone.

"Shit!" Henk said, kicking a metal dustbin. "It knows we're onto it. That might have been the only chance we'll get."

"Wait, hang on," Maria said, her eyes lingering on the galvanised bin as it clattered across the uneven concrete. "It can't have gone far."

The others understood immediately. There were at least three other bins huddled in the corner of the small square area, as well as a stack of wooden pallets and at least seven binbags. They attacked everything in sight. Dave punched a bin and immediately regretted it, shaking his bruised fist off with a wince. Maria kicked the nearest binbag, sending it careening over the back wall into someone's garden. Henk picked up the lid from the bin he'd knocked over and swung it at the pallets.

When none of them reacted, he joined Maria in attacking the binbags.

"RAAA!" Dave stumbled to the side as the final bin threw itself at his shins and rolled away at incredible speed. Again, they gave chase.

If anyone were to be out and about, they would be treated to the sight of three teenagers chasing a runaway bin through the high street, cursing and sweating profusely. "Don't let it get away again!" Henk shouted as the bin hit the side of the curb and flipped end over end through the air.

There was little time to think about what they would do when they caught up to the shapeshifter. Their original plan had been executed flawlessly but still failed to cause anything more than a slight inconvenience to the thing. The bin changed form mid-air, becoming one of the large knives used against it. It rebounded off a lamppost hilt-first and came spinning back towards them. Henk threw himself to the ground at the last second, the deadly projectile whistling over his head. Maria paused to help him up while Dave limped after the weapon, which was now bouncing along the road like a demonic pogo stick.

The knife became a black blur. Then, as Dave reached for it and tumbled to the ground, it was Dave. "What!?" both of them said in unison. "Why does it look like me?" They looked at one another and pushed up to their feet, starting to circle. "Don't listen to it, guys," they said.

"Stand still," Henk ordered as he and Maria got within arm's reach. "Dave. Lift your jumper and show me your stomach."

The real Dave displayed a tattoo of a nun with an electric guitar. As did the fake.

"Tell me this," Maria said, "When I walked in on you in my bathroom last year, what were you doing?"

Mirroring each other's movements, they looked at Henk as if they were unwilling to answer in front of him. Henk folded his arms, said, "Answer her, dude. If I haven't heard of it, it seems like something only the real one would know."

Dave and Dave looked at their feet. "Crying," they both said.

"Well, shit," Maria whispered.

"He was crying?" Henk said. He'd never known his brother to cry, even after their parents killed themselves.

"He made me promise not to say anything. He had bad constipation, and I had to hold his hand and talk him through it."

"Oh. Well, what now?"

"Enough of this," the Daves said. "I'm the real one. LaLaLALA ORPHAN PUPPY BIG FLOPPY WATERMELONS," they screamed, hoping to catch the fake one out.

"Fuck this," Henk said. "We could be here all night."

He walked up to the Dave on the right and slapped him hard across the face. Dave's head whipped to the left, and a tooth (loosed by the earlier elbow) went flying from between his lips. Without pause, Henk delivered another slap, this one to the face of the other Dave. His face warped with the impact, thin tendrils of black gunk splaying out in the direction of the slap. The shapeshifter immediately began to melt itself down to its natural state.

They were not going to let it get away so easily a third time.

Maria gasped as Henk threw himself on top of the slithering mess. It dragged him along the tarmac but was unable to pull him very far. "The petrol!" he screamed as it grew arms varying sizes and started beating at his torso.

"I'll get it on you!" Maria screamed, "It's too dangerous."

"JUST DO IT!"

Dave took a break from trying to wiggle his broken tooth back into the gap in his gums and snatched the hip flask from Maria. He ran to Henk and doused the pair of them without hesitation. "Lighter!"

Maria approached with the zippo while Dave backed away. As soon as Henk rolled clear of the area, she sparked the flame at hurled it at the retreating shapeshifter. It released an otherworldly scream as the fire consumed its body. Henk, Dave and Maria covered their faces as a wave of heat blossomed across the width of the road. The shifter warped rapidly, its core superheated. One second, a burnt-out truck, then a bowling ball. Then it was Maria's father, screaming *WHY?* When the flames began to die out, all that was left was a puddle of bubbling ink and a large swath of burnt road.

Dripping with combustible fluids, Henk shrugged his sodden clothing off and took the jumper offered by Dave. He caught Maria watching him out the corner of his eye but made no attempt to cover his junk. Instead of slipping the jumper over his head, he forced his legs through the arm holes and tightened the top around his waist with the drawstring of the hood.

"Looking good," Maria said with a wink.

"You look like a paedophile," Dave offered.

Maria slapped him playfully on the shoulder. "Gross."

Dave spat a wad of thick crimson to the floor, then gave a weak grin, extended a hand between them, palm down. Maria clapped hers over Dave's, and Henk's landed on top of that.

"SONS OF SORROW!"

Chapter 12

Henk was woken unceremoniously by Dave farting in his face. He smacked his brother's bare ass away and rolled over to face the back of the sofa.

"Wake up, dickhead," Dave said. "Maria's gone."

Henk rubbed the sleep from his eyes and shrugged himself up. "What do you mean, gone?" Dave dropped a piece of paper onto Henk's legs and then drew the curtains. Squinting against the morning sun, Henk brought the note up to his face.

Gone to see a man about a Gimp. Back later.
Maria x

The conversation they'd had the night before came rushing back as he kicked the blanket off his legs. "I can't believe she's gone out without us." Dave remained silent, his back to Henk as he stared up and down the road outside. Henk sighed. "Last night, Maria told me she used to like me. She was angry at us for leaving."

"I know," Dave said without turning to face him.

"What do you mean, you know? You know she was mad at us?"

Dave looked over his shoulder. "I know she used to like you. You knew that too, right?"

Henk shot up. "Are you kidding me right now? You *know* how much I liked Maria, why didn't you say something?"

Dave's body followed his head, giving his full attention. "What did you want me to do? I didn't realise you needed it spelling out to you. It was obvious even *before* she gave you that handy."

Henk shut his eyes and pressed his fingers to his temples. He'd been awake less than a minute and already was getting a tension headache. "Whatever. Okay. Let's just get out of here, shall we? We need to catch up to her before she hurts herself."

"She's survived in Sorrow all these years without our help. But okay, sure. Let's head out on another wild goose chase."

"What else are we going to do? You might be happy to sit around smoking mo-gro, but I'm going to sort this out."

"And be back in time for the wedding."

"Sure. It's time we spoke to the Knob Goblin."

Henk was feeling pretty shitty about the night before. Still, perhaps if he could find Maria's fiancée and make sure they made it to the altar, he might be able to rectify some of the harboured resentment she clearly felt towards him and put it in the past.

The town square was once again a bustle of activity. Children ran screaming from masked attackers with blood-stained machetes. Parents joked and laughed and took photos of their kids being fake-disembowelled. A tall man in a top hat and a black suit walked with a rigid gait along the pavement, his wooden cane clacking against the floor with every other step. Although Henk knew it wasn't the real Pale Groper, he found himself looking away all the same—the memories of that bastard's cold hands on his junk were too much to be dealing with on top of everything else going on.

They left the hubbub heading east, up the steep hill that was Terry Street towards the police station. It was just as Henk remembered it—a small, black building with tiny windows and metal bars across the front door. He reached through the bars and knocked twice.

"Piss off, I'm busy," came the reply.

"It's Henk and Dave. We need to know what you know about the Gimp."

After a moment, the door creaked inward, and Brett's pale face peered out from the darkness within. "Decided you want my help then, hey boys? The 'Sons of Sorrow' a little rusty, are they?"

"Don't call us that," Henk said.

"The fuck are you doing in there, man?" Dave asked, pressing his face to the bars. "And why do you have clamps on your nipples?"

"None of your god damn business," Brett scowled, his initial confidence fast fading. "What's your business with the Gimp?"

"We think it's connected to the Head . . . to the rest of the weird shit that happens around here," Henk said.

From behind Brett came a low, male moan and the sound of flesh slapping against flesh. He raised his voice, "What are you talking about?"

"We found this book. It has pictures of the Head, the Gimp, a shit ton of other—"

"Book? What book?"

"Pastor Wicker had it in some kind of underground vault. He's dead, by the way."

Brett grimaced. "For fucks sake. I told him to burn that damn thing."

"Are you just going to stand there half-naked with your tits tied up, or are you going to let us in so we can talk about this in private?" Dave asked.

Brett's shoulders dropped. He turned away, and there were a couple of clicks as he snapped the clamps from his swollen, purple nips. Then, he unlocked the barred gate and swung it outward. "Hurry."

The station was dark, damp, and stank of sweat and stale semen. Old magazines were strewn across a worn coffee table, crinkled beyond recognition, and two ripped armchairs faced a heavy-looking TV.

"Christ, man. What is wrong with you?"

Brett fumbled for the TV remote and killed the video of the masked man humping a pale-blue woman next to an open grave. "Research. Confiscated evidence."

"Sure." Henk tried to erase the image from his memory before it could take root and flicked the light switch, throwing the room into a pale, sickly glow.

Brett hissed, then reached for his police shirt and buttoned it up while his eyes adjusted to the light. He then hurried about the small room, kicking bunched tissues out of sight. "Did the old fool say anything before he died?"

A vortex of dust shot into the air as Dave slumped into one of the armchairs. Waving it away from his face, Dave said: "He told us about the Head. About the town council. That they fed it sadness. And bodies. That somehow, other entities can coast into our world through its power, several of which we've had the pleasure of dealing with personally. That things are getting worse around here, and the entire town could be in danger."

"That the Gimp is one of those entities," Henk interjected. "And for whatever reason, you've been letting it move about the town as it pleases."

"That's not entirely true."

"What is that supposed to mean?"

Brett sighed. "I tried to tell myself things were not getting worse. For a while, I even managed to convince myself, but all these people that have been going missing . . ."

"What are you trying to tell us?" Henk asked, his patience wearing thin and the overpowering scent of spunk on every surface beginning to make him lightheaded.

"Follow me." Brett started towards the front door but turned left before reaching it and ascended a narrow staircase hidden behind a thin partition wall.

The room was more of a closet than anything else, barely wide enough to admit the three of them. Brett pushed aside a stack of empty cardboard boxes and retrieved a black binbag. Henk and Dave jostled for space as Brett presented it to them.

"What is this?" Dave said, "Couldn't you have just brought it down to us?"

Brett looked to the bag clutched in his shaking hand, then to them. "I suppose."

Dave made to go back downstairs, but Henk put a hand on his shoulder, stopping him. He'd rather be cramped than standing in the Knob Goblin's wank palace. He took the bag from Brett and turned it upside down, shaking the contents to the floor. At first glance, it seemed as if another black bag had fallen out. Then Dave pinched the garment between his thumb and forefinger, lifting it at length as if it were a rotting carcass.

"I killed it a few years back," Brett said.

"Wait, wait. *You're* the Gimp?" Henk said, lifting the head.

"Uh-huh. We had a couple of bodies turn up around town. Faces chewed to the bone. One night, when I was out in the graveyard. Chasing a lead," he hastened to add, ignoring the raised eyebrows, "I saw a glistening black figure dragging a corpse into the woods. Knocked the fucker out with a crack of Ol' Whacky," he motioned to his baton, "then realised what I'd caught."

"You recognised it from the book?"

"I did. I've been privy to the information held in that compendium since joining the police force. Ugly bastard it was, too. Check it out." Brett returned to the stack of cardboard boxes and lifted a large wooden box this time. He snapped the latch and lifted the lid to reveal a red-raw face with hollow eye sockets and two-inch-long teeth.

"Gross! Why have you kept that thing?!" Dave asked, flinching as the face was lifted towards him.

"Why would I get rid of it? It's one of a kind. I don't want to be a cop forever, you know. One day, I'm going to open a museum of curiosities right here in Sorrow. Reckon it'd make a killing, no pun intended, what with all the tourism already here. I've got a couple more if you want to see them?"

"I think I speak for both of us when I say no, thanks. We're good," Henk said. "So, what happened next? Why are you wearing that thing? Or do I not want to know?"

Brett chuckled, wagged a finger in Henk's face. "Good one. Nah. As I said, I knew what the Gimp was, but back then, we hadn't had a single close encounter with the Head. Turns out, the Gimp was feeding the bodies to it all along. After I killed it . . . well, this is speculation on my part, but the Head was not happy that it had to start working harder for its food."

"Are you going to tell us why you've been wearing it or keep dodging the question?" Dave asked.

"I've been feeding it the bodies of the suicides, doing the Gimp's job. It doesn't seem to know I'm not the original."

"You've been doing *what?*" Henk spat. Dave dropped the suit to the floor as if he were afraid it would suddenly possess him.

"I've been studying it. Trying to find out how it works. If it has any weaknesses. Failing that, if there's a way I can shut down its ability to summon other entities. At least a big part of the problem would be dealt with."

Henk shoved Brett without warning. "You've been helping it grow? You're the only thing the people of Sorrow have to call the law. You're supposed to be protecting them! Instead, you've been feeding dead bodies to the fucking thing and allowing tourists to swarm over this place, unaware that it's growing more powerful by the day?"

"N-no . . . I *am* protecting them. By feeding the Head, I'm keeping it satisfied. Don't you see? The Gimp suit provides an opportunity to get closer to it than anyone ever has!"

"He might be onto something, you know," Dave said.

Henk spun to him, eyebrows raised to his hairline, "Don't tell me you're buying this shit?"

"Think about it. If wearing that scabby thing can get us up close and personal with the Head, it could be key to putting it in the ground once and for all. Without it, we wouldn't stand a chance of approaching it."

Henk was unwilling to believe the Knob Goblin may hold the answer to all their problems, but he bit his tongue. What if they were right? He'd be helping no one by letting his pride stand in the way. He'd already decided on some level that he wouldn't be leaving Sorrow again without making sure Maria was going to be okay first. "Shit. Maria. Brett, have you seen her? She left us a note saying she was going to see the Gimp."

"Huh? No . . . she hasn't been to see me at all."

"Well, I guess she didn't know it *was* you," Dave said.

"No, she does," Brett said offhandedly as he crammed the head back into the box. "I told her what I was doing ages ago."

112

"You did?" Henk said, brain starting to melt out his ears. He decided it would be better to put that aside for now. "Did you at least learn anything we don't already know when you were cosplaying as the Gimp? How we can hurt it?"

"I've learnt it cannot be hurt. It can't be poisoned. You don't want to know what I had to do to test that one. Its skin is impenetrable. I know this because my other dad—Bobby—shot it with a shotgun while feeding it a corpse. The bullet exploded on impact, nearly took my eye out, then it retreated under the dirt."

"Where's your other dad now?"

A sudden scream interrupted them. Henk ran to the window to see a tall man with a potato sack over his head chasing a tourist, sharpened pitchfork held in front of him like a spear. The man wound up, then grunted as he released the multi-pronged missile. It stuck in the pocked road surface and reverberated with a metallic twang. After the tourist turned around to snap a quick picture, he ran away giggling like a lovesick schoolgirl. Potato-head retrieved his pitchfork then came back towards the police station. Despite knowing the real Potato-head had passed through the digestive tracts of several of the townfolk when Henk was still young (they'd, unfortunately, missed out on what was supposedly the juiciest potato flesh the town had ever tasted), adrenaline pulsed through his veins as the figure passed out of sight, below the window.

A moment later, "You in, boy?" Then, muttering, "Goddamn waste of space, kid."

"I'm up here, dad."

"You playin' dress-up with that leather suit again?" More muttering, "Frickin' fairy queen motherfucker." Footsteps on the bottom of the stairs.

"We've got civilians here, Dad. Working on a case. We're coming down." Brett nodded toward the staircase for the others to lead the way.

Billy Benderson shuffled into the TV room and tossed his novelty headwear onto one of the armchairs before dropping his skinny ass into the other. He sniffed each armpit in turn. "You're actually doing some work?"

"Dad," Brett tensed as the tall man's eyes widened, "Sir. If what these boys are telling me are true, things are worse than we thought."

Henk resented Brett referring to them as 'boys' but decided to keep his trap shut. The interaction between father and son was simply too surreal to interrupt.

"The corpse diddler struck again, has he?"

Brett gulped audibly, avoiding all eye contact. "No, Sir. Pastor Wicker is dead. Killed by the Head."

"Well technically-" Dave began, but Henk waved him off.

"And we've got more missing persons reports trickling in. Majority of them are tourists. Know the risks and signed the relevant paperwork when they came here, but we should be concerned all the same. It seems as if the Head is getting agitated. If we don't do something soon, we could be dealing with an attack on a scale we've never seen."

Billy Benderson lifted his leg and released a long, whining fart, adding to the already toxic atmosphere. "Forget it, son. We've got a good thing going here, what with all these out of towners chucking their city money our way. Sure, we still get the odd weekly homicide, suicide, or person waking up missing, but it's all par for the course. We leave the Head alone; it leaves us alone. Isn't that what's been working all these years?"

"Perhaps. But we can't be sure of anything concerning the Head . . ."

"You fuckin' second-guessing me, you little bitch? Forget it. Worst comes to worst; a few extra bodies here and there never hurt nobody. Hell, it'll only bring more business our way."

Dave cleared his throat, unable to keep quiet any longer. This time, Henk didn't interrupt—he was impressed his brother had behaved as well as he had so far. Addressing Billy directly, he said, "No wonder so many people die in this town, what with the likes of you running this place. I never thought I'd be siding with the Knob Goblin on anything—and don't take this the wrong way, Brett, but fuck you—but if my friend Maria turns up dead, I'm holding you personally responsible."

"Or Harman," Henk added.

Dave shrugged, "I guess."

Billy chuckled. He leaned forward and snatched a half-drunk bottle of beer with what looked like a cigarette butt floating in it and proceeded to neck the lot. After tossing the empty to the floor and putting his boots up on the coffee table, he said: "Give it a rest. Do you have any idea how many people have come to me over the years with the same empty threats? Sorrow is what

Sorrow is. People don't like it, they know where the door is. I'm too old and too ugly to be fightin' losing battles these days but look, you boys want to play soldiers? That's fine. You can even take my rifle, all I care. The more trouble you cause round here, the more money I'm gonna make in the long run. All I ask is you stay outta my way."

"You're pathetic," Henk said, to which the cop simply shrugged and reached for the TV remote.

Billy almost leapt out of the chair when the TV came on, and the video resumed playing. "Christ's sake, boy. Bobby would be rolling in his grave if he saw this shit. What in the hell is wrong with you?"

"It's evidence!"

Henk tapped Brett on the shoulder and motioned him to the front door. "Next time you get a stiff, can you give us a heads-up? I want to get a look at the Head for myself."

"Gee, I don't know, guys. I mean, if it finds out . . ."

"Come on, Knob Goblin," Dave said. "It's the least you could do for us, considering we've kept your alter ego on the down-low all these years."

Brett fidgeted with his sleeves, uncomfortable with letting the Gimp suit out of his sight, but ultimately knowing he didn't have a choice in the matter.

They left the police station no better off in their search for Maria or Harman than they had been before but at least had a lead on the Head. It was no wonder Brett turned out the way he had, Henk figured, with a father figure like Billy. He could only imagine what Bobby would have been like when he was around—it was well known that he was the worst of the twins. Enough of a troubled childhood to get off on humping grave dirt? Perhaps not, but it was an interesting insight into the psyche of some of Sorrow's longest-standing citizens nevertheless.

Chapter 13

With no actual leads to follow up, they spent the rest of the morning exploring the attractions about the town and visiting old stomping grounds from their teenage years.

First, they stopped by the Jolly Hangman, the only other pub in Sorrow. The Jolly Hangman had long since closed down after an ongoing problem with possessed beer kegs which were found to be preying on unsuspecting drunks, crushing them, and in some cases, drowning the patrons in their frothy amber. The pub had been reopened as part of the town's rejuvenation plans to bring more visitors, and the kegs that had been lying dormant for years had been captured and displayed in bullet-proof glass cells along the wall behind the bar for the visitor's viewing pleasure. Next, they stopped by the old stables. The stables had been converted into a playground, where parents that wanted their children out of their hair for the day could leave them under the supervision of the workers and explore the town without the worry of their spawn turning up dead or missing. Slides, climbing frames, and arcade machines were all themed around the Bloater that had once terrorised the place, swallowing the poor horses that were tied up there whole. The Bloater had been destroyed when a farmer devised a plan involving explosive-stuffed carrots being fed to a horse, which in turn was left to be eaten by the Bloater. Once devoured, the farmer detonated the explosives, and the massive wooden structure was painted a bright gummy-pink, which it remained to this day. Finally, after stopping for a coffee and a pop-up café run by a woman with no face, they went to see the Last Chance Orphanage.

It held fond memories, such as Henk's first black eye and the time Dave got molested by an extremely attractive nun. With the lack of children living in Sorrow as a whole, the Last Chance Orphanage had been converted into a fun house of sorts, but what surprised them most was the way it was themed; The Sons of Sorrow Fun House. Henk, Dave, and Maria's faces were painted across the front of the brick building. Wide-eyed, open-mouthed, comical depictions made them look more like circus clowns than anything else. Although the interior layout of the building remained similar to how they remembered it, each of the bunk rooms had been gutted. Instead of bunk beds and wardrobes, the rooms were now home to depictions of battle scenes of the monsters they'd defeated over the years. They found (poorly crafted) wax sculptures of themselves facing off against the Spectre in the reading room, laser pens trained on the shadowy figures reaching for them. Their old bunk room was home to the Shapeshifter, depicted as a wolf with seven legs (which never actually happened in real life). The wax models were hunched, hands out in front of them as if to calm the snarling beast.

But it was the final area that threw Henk off. After passing through a hall of mirrors and a maze of fake doors, they found themselves in the Mistress' office, a spacious room that had been primarily used to dole out spankings. There was a gigantic corkboard splayed across the back wall. On the board was a black and white photo of each of the kids that had stayed at the Last Chance Orphanage, along with several throwing darts. This came as no surprise to either of them, for it had always been there. The Mistress' desk and the beanbags (the only thing the kids could sit on after visiting the office) had been stripped out. The room now only had one piece of furniture; a raised wooden platform in the centre held a rather impressive miniature scale recreation of the town, complete with craft trees and little plastic people.

"How did they know about that?" Henk asked, extending a shaky finger to a small field northeast of the town. A single plastic figure with a long, plaited beard stood before what could be mistaken for a pink boulder unless you knew better. As far as Henk was aware, no one else around at that time could have possibly known it was where he'd encountered the Head. Studying the miniature town further, he noticed at least ten other 'Heads' around the place. In each area it had been sighted?

"Maria must have told them," Dave said. "Probably the same way they were able to write a book about us, and whatever else they've done."

Henk wasn't convinced. Something about it just rubbed him the wrong way. Maria knew how much that episode had fucked him up. He couldn't imagine she would have told anyone else about it. "I don't think they should be including that thing as part of the attraction," he said. "Not only do we not know what it's fully capable of, but it's still an active threat."

Henk took each of the miniature head models and shoved them in his pocket.

"We should probably do something about that, too," Dave said.

Henk followed his gaze and saw a giant poster of the Head on the wall next to the door they'd come in from.

VISIT SORROW! It proclaimed. Then, below the photograph of the Head: HOME TO THE WORLD'S COOLEST BIOLOGICAL ANOMALY!

He didn't know what was worse—that the colourful poster was quite clearly aimed at children or that it was improbable to be one of a kind. "We might not be able to destroy all evidence of that fucking thing, but it's a start." Henk tore the poster from the wall and ripped it into tiny pieces, which he then scattered over the room. When he finished, he was hyperventilating, could feel the years of pent-up emotion coming out. It felt good to have something to direct it at.

When he turned to leave, he realised he was being watched by a young boy and an older man. "Dad! It's them!" the boy cried. "The wax people!" The boy went to lift a town map and a pen towards Henk and Dave, but his father held him back.

The man's upper lip lifted in disgust, "Not now, Teddy. Your mother is probably wondering where we are."

"Good one," Dave said as the tourists hurried away.

"I don't give a shit about them," Henk growled. "I didn't ask for any of this, and I don't want it," he stormed into the room next door and put his fist through a wax work figure that could either have been himself or a deformed alien that looked

121

vaguely like him. "Anyway, don't they need our permission to use our likeness?"

Dave shrugged, keeping a safe distance from his irate brother. "I guess it is a little shitty. They probably should have, but I think it's rather cool, in all honesty. We're famous, and we didn't even know it!"

Henk hammer-fisted wax-Dave, causing the real one to flinch. "Cool?! Have you noticed that it's just been one mess up after the next ever since we got off that train? I feel like I'm going insane over here, and you're just plodding along having the time of your life!"

"Dude, you need to take a few deep breaths right now. Try and enjoy yourself. It's not every day we find out we have an entire building dedicated to us. Just try and forget the Head for now."

Henk grit his teeth, struggling, and ultimately failing to contain another outburst. "That's easy for you to say when all you ever want to do is get high! How about you pull your head out your ass for one FUCKING hour and help me understand what the FUCK is going on around here?"

"I don't know how to say this without you taking it the wrong way, but would you consider having a joint *with* me? As you say, it's obviously helping me keep calm."

Henk finished obliterating the wax sculptures under the heel of his shoe and was about to reply when they heard movement.

"Going to investigate the noise now," came the voice of a spotty teenage boy wearing a *Sons of Sorrow Fun House* shirt as he made his way through the end of the false door maze.

The worker poked his head into the room. Henk and Dave took the wax sculptures positions, holding perfectly still. "Huh. Must have been the wind," he muttered as he left again.

"Fuck it. It's not like we have anything else to do right now," Henk said. As much as he didn't want to admit Dave was right, in this particular situation, he may have been. Sure, both Harman and Maria were missing. And sure, the Knob Goblin had been dressing up to feed corpses to the Head. But perhaps getting a little mo-gro would make him care about all of that a little less and enable him to enjoy himself even a fraction of the amount Dave was.

He followed Dave back through the maze of false doors, then the crazy mirrors. Past their bunk room and countless gawping tourists, several of which asked for photos and signatures and were subsequently ignored. Past the spotty teen that had come to check on the wrecked room upstairs, who watched them leave with a cocked eyebrow as if slowly coming to understand he'd been hoodwinked. Finally, back outside.

They found a quiet spot away from the majority of the crowds, sat in the shadow of a boarded-up house, and sparked up a roll of mo-gro.

Chapter 14

Case Four: The Gloved King. October 19th, 2010

Almost two years after vanquishing the Shapeshifter back to wherever-the-fuck dead shapeshifters go, there was a new killer in town. The team had been searching for the Gloved King—as the local paper was calling him—for the last few days to no avail and were beginning to think the vicious murders could have been committed by someone passing through when they saw the bloodied ribbon of skin laying at the side of the road. "Yo . . ." Dave trailed off as he lifted the sagging flesh with the end of a stick.

"Looks like we've found our killer," Maria said.

The Gloved King earned the moniker after the child of a victim survived by hiding in a kitchen cupboard and described the assailant to the authorities. A crude sketch had been mocked up (by none other than Billy Benderson) and plastered about town. Everyone agreed that the man bore more than a slight resemblance to Michael Jackson. Now, the heavily modified face was not something you would be comfortable finding in your kitchen in the dead of night, but this entity, this 'Gloved King', took things up a notch. Like MJ, the assailant wore a white glove on one hand, only the Gloved King would be more than happy to remove it to attack its victims with inch-long talons. The autopsy reports seemed to correlate with the statement given to police by the unnamed child, and it was then that the Sons of Sorrow decided to get involved.

The trail of shredded skin led them further up the road to the Silver Spoon Theatre. The place was temporarily closed following the imposed curfew until the current murderer was dealt with. Still, someone had obviously forgotten to tell The Gloved King, as he had sliced through the padlock securing the front entrance and left it wide open.

"After you," Dave said, gesturing Henk and Maria inside with a theatrical arm sweep.

"Gentleman," Maria replied with more than a hint of sarcasm.

The lobby was lit by several ornate wall lamps and a vast, cube-like lighting structure that ran floor-to-ceiling in front of a sweeping staircase to the upper level. To the left was the closed ticket booth, and dead ahead, below the raised balcony, was a red-carpeted corridor that would take them through to the auditorium. Henk addressed Maria, "Dave and I will take the ground floor. You take the upper balcony. Until we know what we're dealing with, it would be a good idea to have one of us stay out of sight."

"And you think it should be me because I'm the girl, and I need to be protected?"

"Something like that, yeah."

Maria poked him playfully in the throat. "Fine. But only because I can't say no to those eyes."

"Get a room, you two," Dave said. "Preferably *after* we've taken care of this bastard."

Maria rolled her eyes. "I'll be watching, boys. Try not to die."

They waited until Maria had ascended the stairs and was waiting by the doors to the upper circle of the auditorium before they started down the short corridor. Similar to previous cases, they were unsure what to expect once they found this entity. The unnamed child had witnessed both her parents being torn like wet paper by the Gloved King while he grabbed his crotch and made a series of high-pitched whines. It was unclear if this was the extent of its power or if it was capable of far worse. One other detail was cause for concern: none of the murder scenes showed any sign of forced entry. Somehow, the Gloved King was able to enter and exit the properties without leaving any evidence, which is why some of the victims were already in the beginning stages of decomposition by the time they were discovered.

"Ready?" Dave said as he wrapped his hand around the door's handle.

"Hang on." Henk pressed his ear to the surface. Muffled bass could be heard through the thick wood. "We might be able to use the music to our advantage. Try and keep a low profile until we know exactly where he is."

Dave nodded, then opened the door. The music stopped. "HOLY FUCKBALLS."

And just like that, the element of surprise was lost.

Henk couldn't blame his brother for the outburst—the scene that greeted them was not something they had been prepared for.

Although several spotlights lit the stage, it appeared empty. It was the shadows dotted about the seating areas that demanded their attention. Sat throughout the auditorium were at least ten individuals facing the stage. The tops of their exposed skulls were stained black in the low lighting, and the shallow gouges that ran across them were clear as day. Hesitant to take his eyes from the stage, Henk approached the nearest and saw the man had been flayed open from neck to ankle, his nude body one giant party streamer. The seat beneath the corpse did not appear to have collected his bodily fluids, which indicated the attack had occurred elsewhere before the corpse was moved.

Dave was standing over a woman on the other side of the walkway, also scalped, naked, and flayed beyond recognition. The skin hung from her torso like paper through a shredder.

The music started up again. The melody of a synthesiser soon joined the rhythmic bass lick, then drums, and a guitar. Finally, after what could only be described as a series of high-pitched *hee-hee's,* a smoke machine fogged the stage, and the spotlights began to flicker on and off in a line. Henk and Dave stood where they were, transfixed, bobbing their heads in time to the beat and almost enjoying themselves. The music rose to a crescendo. Then the lights went out. Three seconds later, they all came back on, and the music dropped the dirtiest bassline either of them had ever heard. They found themselves unable to do anything but throw their hands up and dance.

On the stage, in the clearing smoke in front of a grotesque dance troupe, stood the Gloved King. The thin man wore a pressed red shirt and black suit trousers. A black fedora partially obscured his face. The disturbing creature spun on his heel, then kicked his head foot out to the side, snapped it back in before performing a backwards slide with both feet. He then reached up with his gloved hand, tilted the fedora back onto his head, and winked at the two dancing in the aisle.

Henk was somewhat aware of the danger they were in. Although the music was slapping, it hurt the very marrow in his bones to try and do anything other than what his body was doing of its own accord. It felt good to dance. His blood pulsed in time with the beat, forcing his limbs to move. He performed a slut drop then started twerking against Dave's leg. Dave responded by spanking his ass and swinging an invisible lasso over his head. He thought he might have heard Dave screaming something over the music, but it was impossible to tell.

There was only the music.

Music was the only thing that mattered. It was so obvious now. Nothing else mattered. Not the flayed corpses that were dancing with the Gloved King on the stage, their skin flaps lifting and splaying out with every twist and turn. Not the Gloved King miming pulling a rope, dragging them slowly towards him as if it were a physical object. It didn't even matter that the Gloved King was on the stage one moment, then snapped his un-gloved fingers and was standing in the aisle ahead of them the next.

The Gloved King bopped his head along with Henk and Dave, his curly, shoulder-length black hair swaying with hypnotic gait. He was smiling at them, and Henk found himself looking into the man's dark eyes and smiling back. His features could cut glass, and for a moment, were enough to pull Henk out of his haze and remind him that this entity was something alien, otherworldly, and incredibly dangerous. But still, he was powerless to do anything but dance, his neck on fire as he tried to pull his head away. If only he could succeed with that, he hoped the rest of his body would follow.

But he couldn't.

Next to him, Dave was in a similar state of distress. A puddle was forming around his feet, slapping wetly with each kick and spin his body performed, a smirk still cemented to his frozen face despite his eyes being wide with terror. His teeth ground together violently, breaking two and damaging several others.

The Gloved King began snapping his fingers in time to the beat, each snap bringing him a few inches closer until he was near enough for them to smell his rancid breath. Only then did he stop and lift his gloved hand. Although reports had stated the glove was white, today it was silver, sparkling, perhaps to commemorate the special occasion of being the one to take down the Sons of Sorrow.

He peeled the glove off.

The flesh of his fingers stopped at the first knuckle, where it mutated to several inches of flexible bone. The ends of each finger were whittled down to razor-thin blades, perfect for separating meat. Within minutes, they would be dancing up on stage with the rest of the flayed troupe.

"AAAAAAIIIIIIIIIIII!!" A fast-moving weight fell from above and landed directly on top of the degloved bastard, bringing him to the ground. "DIE!"

Maria righted herself before the entity had a chance to shake the stars from his eyes. She wrapped both hands around his head and smashed the back of his skull against the polyamide flooring repeatedly. Each hit was delivered with an increasingly satisfying crunch. The other two danced over them, unable to warn Maria as the Gloved King brought its bone-hand up and slashed her across the arm.

She released her grasp on the enemy with a wail, giving him just enough time to get his other hand free and snap its fingers, disappearing from beneath her and reappearing back on stage. Maria used the side of the nearest seat to pull herself upright. The Gloved King spun three-sixty, tipped his fedora back over his face, and started with the *hee-hee's* again.

Henk managed to force his lips apart long enough to say: "Cuvuh yu eees." Not exactly the message he'd been trying to get across, but fortunately, Maria seemed to understand what was going on and had slammed her hands over her ears the moment the bastard tipped his fedora. She ran down the centre aisle of the auditorium with determination, although whatever she was planning was unclear. With her hands disabled, unable to defend herself, she was surely heading to her death. However, instead of mounting the stairs to the stage and the dancing morgue, she took a left at the end of the aisle and made a beeline for the large booth that held the controls for the sound and lighting. The Gloved King was too wrapped up in his dance moves to notice anything was amiss until the auditorium fell silent.

Henk and Dave dropped to the floor, panting and covered in piss. The flayed bodies behind the Gloved King crumpled, motionless. The entity raised his fedora once more and snarled between thin lips, clicked its fingers in a steady cadence, and the bodies rose back to their feet, then continued further, clearing the floor. Useless limbs hung at their sides, as did their ripped lengths of pale skin. As the Gloved King threw his head back and unleashed an ear-piercing *hee-hee*, the bodies took flight.

The brothers threw themselves into the rows of seating as cold hard corpses smashed into their surroundings, wrapping themselves around the backs of chairs and exploding on contact with the floor. Henk peeked out in time to see the Gloved King falling face-first to the stage floor.

Maria stood over the body, clutching her bloodied arm. A snapped microphone stand protruded several feet from the back of the Gloved King's skull. His dying nerves were still twitching by the time Henk and Dave climbed the steps to the side of the stage.

"You saved us," Henk said, putting his hands on his knees and struggling to catch his breath.

Maria shrugged, the teasing glint in her eye never fading. "You would have done the same for me."

"Yeah . . . but that was some serious superhero shit back there," Dave said. He turned to look at the upper circle and the drop that separated it from the ground below.

"Well, you'd already pissed yourself. I wasn't waiting until you followed through."

Dave blushed.

Henk was in utter awe of Maria. She'd single-handedly taken down the Gloved King. He missed Dave's witty response and only realised he was staring at her, lost in himself, when she pushed her breasts together and said: "Want a picture, Henk?"

In typical Henk fashion, he laughed awkwardly and mumbled an apology. If he'd not turned away from her so quickly out of embarrassment, he may have picked up on the fact she was attempting to flirt in her own awkward way. And was now checking out his butt.

There was a bone-chilling crunch as Dave wiggled the mic stand free of the Gloved King's skull, and a spurt of black brain matter sprayed across his piss-soaked shoes. "What should we do with the body?"

"Leave it for the cops," Maria said. "And the stand."

"What about your prints? I know we're doing the town a service, but surely it'd be easier not to have any ties to a murder scene. There's a lot of bodies here . . ."

"Sure. But then someone else would claim the glory, wouldn't they? In case you hadn't realised, the cops around here don't exactly care too much about the details. As long as the culprit is either dead or jailed, they're happy."

"Maria's not wrong," Henk said, having gotten over his earlier shame (although still unable to look her in the eye). "Although it might be nice to live somewhere without the constant danger one day. I can live without glory."

"You'd never leave me," Maria said. Something about her hunched posture gave the impression the statement was a test. "Would you?"

"Of course not," Henk said. "You could come with me! And you, Dave."

Dave looked up from picking a scab on his elbow. "Huh?"

"Forget it. But before too long, we'll have enough to leave this place behind for good, and I, for one, cannot wait."

"Right on, man," Dave said, although it was clear he was already no longer paying attention.

Had Henk been even a little better at picking up on body language, he might have realised right then that Maria had never had the intention of leaving town. Perhaps she never even thought Henk was serious about it. Or even if he was, that he would follow through with it.

But Henk had never been great at sharing his true feelings. The sadness that was eating him from the inside, or the visions of his parents that kept him up at night. He had to be strong not only for himself but for the rest of their group. Girls didn't like sensitive guys, as far as he was aware? He was reluctant to ruin any chance he may or may not have with her by babbling like a baby, but it did not come without a cost—he was reluctant to let any emotion show, should it cause a fissure in the dam that was holding the rest of him together.

Chapter 15

Henk and Dave had spent the better part of an hour wrestling with the limbs they'd grown from the mo-gro. Dave's grew between his shoulder blades, an arm with long, hairy fingers. Henk had a third leg, which had sprouted from his throat, complete with a dainty foot and red painted toenails. Plus, from the elbow down, his arms were a covered in a writhing blanket of fingers. Despite this, he was feeling a little better. The mo-gro had dulled both his mind and his muscles, making everything seem a little less critical.

Dave was right—Maria had survived this long without them around, so why would anything have changed now he was back? Answer: it hadn't. He was practically dozing off when Dave suggested, "Maybe we should head back to Maria's? She might have gone home and wondered where we are."

Henk lifted his head from his knees and rubbed his eyes. He was still relatively baked and would be for the next few hours. He wasn't worried about the extra appendage (or the fingers) as they would disappear along with the high. "Yeah, okay. Wouldn't mind a nap when we get there."

They took the side roads, avoiding the main square and the shocked stares of those visiting that may be unfamiliar with the drug and its side effects. There were still a few tourists milling around, taking selfies outside Madam Bouvier's House of Skin, peering through cracks in the windows of boarded-up houses. Still, those that saw them seemed to assume they were just another pair of costumed entertainers. They got the odd half-look or pointing kid as they passed, Henk's thin leg bouncing off his chest and Dave's hand massaging his own shoulders, but he was too stoned to care. In fact, he imagined they must look quite funny.

Dave knocked on Maria's door with his third arm. After waiting no more than five seconds, he tried the handle and found it unlocked. "Coooeee," he called. "Mariaaaa?" Henk giggled, followed him inside. After a quick sweep of the house, it became clear Maria had not yet returned home, or if she had, hadn't left any kind of message to let them know what was going on. "What now?"

"Now? Now we nap," Henk said, heading to the front room and flopping onto the sofa. "Wake me up when my leg's gone."

Dave saluted with his extra arm. "I'm probably going to roll another. You're more than welcome to join."

Henk waved him off. His eyes were heavy. He wanted to get rid of the leg, not grow a fourth. He heard Dave perch on the edge of the armchair opposite and remove his rolling equipment. A moment later, he left the room and exited the house via the back door to smoke in Maria's garden.

"Dude, WAKE UP!"

Henk had fallen asleep instantly, and it took him a moment to realise the fingers that had covered Dave's face were real. He shut his eyes again. "Ugh. Sleeping."

"Seriously, man, you have to wake up NOW. You need to see this. I'm not fucking around."

Henk rubbed his face and sat up. It was hard to take his brother seriously with a mess of fingers wriggling where his features should be, but he could tell something was wrong. The last time he'd seen his brother this serious was when he told Henk their parents had been found. "What's going on?"

"You need to see this for yourself," was all he said as he led Henk to the back door and out to the modest garden. He pointed to a sheet of tarpaulin covering the pond. There was nothing suspicious about it—Maria had explained it was there to stop the birds from taking her Lucky Charms, which is the name she'd given her koi. "I thought I'd give them some food, you know? Can't be nice trapped under there in the dark all day."

Henk flopped his extra leg over his head and used his free hand to lift the blue plastic. "You fuck," he muttered, flinching away instinctively. "You could have warned me there was a body under there." Henk took the tarp by the corner and dragged it away from the pond. The nude body had been wedged into the small wet hole without any sign of respect. Two fat koi slapped desperately in the shallow pool of water between the corpse's bloated stomach and the surface of the pond. The body had little breasts and hairy nipples, and for a terrifying moment, Henk thought it might have been Maria . . . until the fish managed to dive beneath the off-pink legs and a small mushroom-headed penis drifted lazily to the surface. The corpse's head had been bent back behind the shoulders, and Henk made space for Dave and his three arms to grab hold of the man's shoulders and waist to wriggle it free. They dragged it out of the pond together.

"Pig boy," Dave whispered.

"Harman," Henk said, figuring the least they could do was call him by his real name.

"Can't believe we've been wasting our time looking for him, and he's been here all along," Dave said. He picked up the joint he'd dropped when he found the body and relit it.

"And Maria has gone. . ."

Dave exhaled, and a nostril began to form on his wrist. "What are you trying to say? That Maria did this?"

"I don't know what to think anymore. Last night, when you went to bed, I saw a side of her I've never seen before."

"So?" The tip of a nose began to form on Dave's wrist.

"I don't know. Something hasn't felt right since we got here." Henk shoved his hands in his pockets and remembered they were full of the miniature Heads. He tossed them into the pond. "All I'm saying is I wouldn't be surprised if she knows more than she's letting on. This is her house . . ."

Dave flicked the mo-gro butt into the pond. It was immediately swallowed by a koi, which grew an eye on the top of its head. "Well, yeah. That much is obvious, what with the orphanage and what the Knob Goblin was saying . . . hang on. You know what this means, don't you?" A smile spread across his face as he pointed at the body.

"No, man. Not Harman. This . . . he could be evidence."

"Fuck that. This is exactly what we need to get close to it!"

Dave returned to the house with the Knob Goblin in tow twenty minutes later. Henk had inspected the corpse as much as he cared to but could see no obvious cause of death. Aside from the knife wound below his left ear. But he was no doctor, so that was neither here nor there. "Not you, too," Brett said as he entered the back garden and set eyes on Henk. "I was hoping at least one of you would have had the sense to stay away from the mo-gro."

Henk shrugged and tossed his throat-leg over his shoulder.

Brett open-palmed his forehead. Then, he turned his attention to the body, lifted his chin towards the pond. "You say you found him in there?"

"Yeah. I'm guessing it was only meant to be temporary," Henk said.

Brett crouched alongside the corpse, ran his hands along the bare flesh, feeling for anything unusual.

"We didn't bring you here to fuck it," Dave said.

Brett scowled in response.

"Did you bring it?"

"Of course," Brett snapped. He stood and slid the bag from his shoulder, tipping the contents to the grass. He looked to Henk, "I suppose you'll be the one wearing it. There's something you should know before you put it on, though."

138

"Ugh. What have you been doing in it?"

"No," Knob Goblin growled, "can we just stop with the corpse-fucking jokes now?"

Neither brother agreed. Henk was thankful he was not a necrophiliac.

Brett picked the gimp suit up by the shoulders and held it out. "When you put it on, things might look a little funny. Try not to freak out. It's all part of whatever power the original Gimp had."

"Funny how? Like ha-ha funny? Or I'm going to try and tear my eyes out and stamp on them kind of funny?"

Brett thrust the suit into Henk's hands. "Just put it on and see for yourself. Once you've gotten used to it, we can figure out how we're going to get this body out to the Head."

Henk shook his head, unsatisfied with Brett's explanation, but started stripping off regardless.

"You know where it is right now then?" Dave asked. The nose on his wrist, now fully formed, was leaking yellowy fluid from both nostrils. He wiped it on his trousers.

"No. But Henk will, as soon as he's in the suit. I'd usually use a wheelbarrow to get the bodies out to it, but . . . I don't see one around here. And given that it's broad daylight, we might look a little suspicious."

"So, how're we doing this?" Henk asked. He'd wedged his body into the suit and shrugged the tight latex over his shoulders. All that was left was the headpiece, which was proving to be challenging to cram his extra leg into. Dave held the headpiece while Henk pinned the leg over the top of his head and down the back of his neck, but still, the black latex would not stretch enough.

"Depends on where it is at the moment. Once we know that, we can start to worry about transport."

"It's not going to fit," Dave said, releasing the material with a loud *twang!*

"We might have to cut it off," Brett said.

The leg started kicking in defiance, smacking Henk repeatedly in the chest. He wrapped both hands around the ankle to prevent it from moving. "Fuck no," he said. "I can tell you've never done mo-gro. This thing grew out of me. I can feel everything it can."

"Well, the only other option is to leave it dangling through the mouth hole, but I'm not sure the Head won't realise something is different about the Gimp if it sees you like that."

"It's either that or we wait until he sobers up," Dave said.

"It'll be fine," Henk said. "It's a giant fucking head. I doubt an extra leg is going to throw it off." He was reluctant to say that the only reason he agreed to this in the first place was that he was baked. If he were sober, chances are he wouldn't want to get anywhere near the thing.

And so, Henk bent the leg up once again, only this time, instead of trying to tuck it in behind him, he pushed the foot through the suit's rubber-lipped mouth before threading the rest of the thin leg through. The headpiece came down over his face and became flush with the neck. "WHATINTHEFUCK," he screamed, clawing at the rubber and wrenching it free from his face.

"I told you not to freak out," Brett said. "I think it's how *they* see our town. Don't worry, though. It's perfectly safe."

Henk looked to Dave, lost for words. Dave merely shrugged and flicked snot from his wrist-nose. If he weren't so short, Henk would have insisted his brother wear the suit instead. Reluctantly, Henk snapped the mask over his face once again.

Orange. The sky was orange. The floor was orange. The fish swimming about the pond were orange. Actually, they were already orange. But they were MORE ORANGE. Henk squeezed his eyes shut to give himself a moment to process the vivid colour before it fried his retinas like two miniature egg yolks.

He opened his eyes.

Brett was a rabbit. A giant, black, fuzzy, razor-toothed rabbit. His goofy mouth opened, and he produced a sound like a thousand sins. Henk had no idea how he knew what a thousand sins sounded like. He just *did.*

Dave was still Dave. Only he was composed entirely of polystyrene. His thin lips rubbed against one another, producing a scratchy-rubbing noise. Gone were his clothes, features, any distinguishing qualities, replaced by rigid cellular plastic.

The black of Brett's fur and the white of Dave's *everything* seemed to bring more colour into this new world. Thin tendrils of neon drifted from their unnatural bodies, spinning, rising, bleeding in all directions until the orange was almost entirely replaced by vibrant greens, blues, and purples.

Brett said something else, which sounded like the mating call of an orca, but Henk was unable to respond. Not only was the extra leg blocking the mouth hole and forcing him to breathe

141

through two tiny pin-prick holes for his nose, but words just didn't seem to be able to form inside his head. It was as if his brain were overloaded by stimuli, able to operate solely at base level, shutting off parts it deemed unessential while allowing him to continue processing image, sound, and movement.

Then he saw it. The Head. A pulsing sky-blue shadow in the far distance, visible through the walls of Maria's house (which was now continuously melting and rebuilding itself) and countless other buildings that should have stood in the way. He tried to tell the others what he saw, but the best he could do was point. Then, he peeled the tight material from his face once more and took in a deep breath of fresh air as the world returned to normality.

"Pretty messed up, huh?" Brett said with a smirk. "What was I? A dragon? A bloodthirsty lion?"

"You were a rabbit," Henk said, shaking the last of the colour from his eyes. Brett looked disappointed with his answer, so he added, "With giant razor teeth and the breath of sin."

"Fuck yeah."

"And you were a little polystyrene mannequin," he said to Dave. "Whatever the hell that means. Anyway, the Head is over there," he said, pointing once again. "Across town. But I'm not putting this shit back on until I absolutely have to."

"There's only one option, then." Brett took the walkie talkie from his belt of useless implements and held down the 'talk' button. "Squad car one, come in squad car one."

A moment later there was a crackle of static, followed by a tired voice: "Go ahead."

"Squad car one, this is Officer Brett Benderson of Sorrow PD requesting pickup at 224 Rookery Road, over."

"Sure thing, Brett. But you still owe me from the last time."

"Roger that, squad car one. What is your ETA?"

"Five minutes out."

"Rodger dodger tango one-two-seven over and out." He clipped the radio back onto his belt.

"Fucking dork," Dave said without malice.

Brett pretended he hadn't heard him. He enjoyed being the only one with official authority, no matter how little it stood for anything around there. "We should get this body through the house and ready for pickup."

Dave took Harman's upper body, utilising all three of his arms. The wrist-nose dribbled snot down the corpse's face. "Isn't he going to wonder why one of us is dressed in a gimp suit while transporting a dead body?"

"Don't forget the limbs," Henk added, taking Harman's left leg in his rubbery hands while Brett took the right.

"Not at all," Brett said. "Not only is my driver reliable, but he's also professional and prides himself on his discretion."

Chapter 16

"I wouldn't normally say nothin', Officer Benderson, what with you being the law and all, but why in the hell's name are you moving a body with two multi-limbed freaks? One of which is dressed in a gimp suit, no less."

"Hey, Jenk," Dave said, waving with three arms. "Didn't realise you were on the payroll, too."

"I'm not." Jenk pouted, then rolled his eyes as if he'd had enough already. Then, to Brett, "These two I can ignore, but just what makes you think I'm going to put a dead guy in my car?"

"It's official police duty, and if you're unwilling to cooperate, then I'll have to commandeer your vehicle," Brett said.

"Come on, son. You know as well as I do that I'm stuck in this damn contraption. I ain't going nowhere. So, the way I see it, you'd better be greasing my palm something fine if you want me to get anywhere near that stinking thing."

Henk and Dave were already at the back of the car, ready to lift Harman's body into the boot. Henk had no idea how he would explain what was going on to Maria if she were to show up. He was beginning to sober, could feel the leg starting to shrink, and was therefore starting to realise the absurdity of the situation.

"Fine," Brett said. He lowered his voice and bent to the driver's window. "One crime."

"Three," the driver countered.

"Two, final offer."

Jenk pretended to consider this offer for a moment before saying, "Deal."

"No murders, though, okay? We've got enough of that going around."

"I ain't no murderer, son." He looked visibly offended by the comment, but Henk couldn't help but notice his sausage-link fingers were crossed. Or perhaps they were stuck that way, welded into position from years of being cramped into the vehicle.

The boot was packed. Several bags of lime, some rope, and a shovel. It seemed more likely the driver's fingers were crossed intentionally, although just how he would bury a body was anyone's guess. "There's no room," Henk said to Brett.

Brett 'volunteered' to sit in the front alongside Jenk, semi-smothered by the folds of flab that filled the space, which left Henk sharing the back seat with Dave, and Harman in the middle, riding bitch. They'd not noticed how bad the slimy corpse smelled before being forced into a tin can shoulder-to-shoulder, a curious blend of algae and that dead fox that one of the kids in the orphanage had left in Dave's bed when they were younger. Harman's swollen head flopped onto Dave's shoulder as the car took off. Dave shrugged it off onto Henk's, who shouldered it back to Dave. This went on for the majority of the journey. Brett eventually suggested Henk put the mask on again to get a more precise destination.

This time, when the leather suctioned itself to his face, Henk's bowel almost voided. Not only was he crammed into a free-falling vehicle with a giant demented rabbit and a polystyrene man, but the driver had transformed into a weeping mass of blinking eyeballs.

"Hey, bro," said a phlegmy voice, "where we going?"

Harman was talking. His head was flopped over his right shoulder towards Henk once again, but his eyes were now open, looking up at him. Henk pushed himself as far against the door as he could and stared at the pale man, who for whatever reason still looked like himself, only more alive.

Harman stared as if awaiting a response.

Henk mumbled against the leg: "We're going to see the Head."

"We are? Why? Isn't it dangerous?"

"It is. But that's exactly why we're going. We have to look for a weakness."

The polystyrene man turned his head to Henk and screamed something in scratches.

"Well, I guess that explains the gimp suit," Harman said. "Wait, why are you taking me, though? You're not going to feed me to it, are you!?"

"It's the only way," Henk muttered. He was well aware that he was making unintelligible noises right now, and the others were probably looking at him like he was crazy, but he didn't care. He was reasonably certain he *was* crazy. "I'm sorry."

Harman's eyes flitted wildly as if looking for an escape. "Please. I'll do anything. I don't want to die."

"You're already dead. That's the point."

"I thought something was wrong . . ."

Henk took a moment to look around for the Head, saw its blue outline pulsing ahead and to the right. He pointed, and the car turned. He tried to ignore the bright-pink tsunami roaring across the top of the houses, telling himself it wasn't real. "Sorry, buddy, but it's not all bad. Now that you're able to talk, do you know who killed you?"

"I was murdered? I . . . I don't know." He sounded defeated as if being able to finger his killer would somehow bring him back to life.

Henk removed the mask once more and watched the life disappear from Harman's eyes.

"What was that about?" Dave asked. "You were speaking in tongues."

"Don't worry about it," Henk said, relieved to see the driver was no longer a writhing mass of eyes. Jenk's almost equally unappealing appearance was restored, his mass almost consuming the Knob Goblin entirely.

"This is as far as I can go," Jenk said as he pulled the vehicle up alongside a wooden gate. Beyond was nothing but fields for miles. Henk realised where they were straight away.

"Isn't this where you saw it last time?" Dave asked as they lifted the corpse from the car and dropped it on the other side of the fence.

"It is." Henk massaged his throat-leg, willing it to hurry up and shrink. The gimp suit was sobering him further, leaving him much more self-conscious of the fact he had a female leg on his head. "Maybe it's only able to go to certain places."

147

"That would explain how they knew where to put the mini Heads in the model village," Dave offered.

"Correct-a-mondo," Brett said, placing his hands on his hips in what he surely hoped was a power stance. "The Head travels between twelve locations in and around Sorrow, only moving on when there are people within a certain vicinity of it. Which is why the suit could be key to being rid of it once and for all."

They asked Jenk to wait before climbing the gate and stepping into the field beyond. Brett and Dave helped Henk move the body a short way up the path until they reached the top of a decline. "You're on your own from here," Brett said. "Get that mask on and make sure it stays on until you're clear."

"So . . . what do I do when I get down there?" Henk asked.

"Just feed it the body. It's always hungry, so there shouldn't be any problems."

"Shouldn't be?"

The Knob Goblin held out his left hand. His pinky finger was missing, and a purple scar ran along the top of the second knuckle and down the side of his hand. "Just watch your hands."

"Good luck, buddy," Dave said, sparking yet another joint of mo-gro.

Henk took one last breath of fresh air and stretched the mask back over his face.

"Where'd you go? Where are we?"

Henk did his best to ignore Harman's questions as he took him by the wrists and started to drag him through the long grass down the hill, but it was hard to pretend he couldn't hear him when he was practically face to face with the guy.

"Just leave me here. No one will have to know. I won't tell."

Henk looked over his shoulder, still no sign of the Head.

"Henk, please, listen to me. You don't have to do this. What could you possibly have to gain by feeding me to it? Please, think of Maria."

"Maria doesn't have to know," Henk replied.

"What will you tell her, then? Are you happy to let her believe I ran out on her before the wedding? Got cold feet?"

"You do have cold feet. And hands. And everything else."

"You know what I mean."

The decline levelled out, and Henk dropped Harman's arms. He arched backwards to ease a little of the tension dragging the body was putting on his spine. Not far to go; the gentle trickle of the river could be heard beyond the bushes. Just a little further, and he would be face to face with the thing that had been plaguing him for years. "Nearly there, old buddy."

"It's not too late," Harman pleaded as Henk resumed dragging.

"I'm sorry, mate. I really am. But you're already dead. If it weren't this, you'd either be stuffed in a wooden box and buried to rot away or stuffed in a wooden box and burned to cinders. At least this way, your death will mean something."

"I don't want to be dead. Take me to the hospital, there might be a way . . . what are you doing?" he said as Henk dropped his arms and crouched alongside him. A moment later, he found himself face-down in the dirt.

Henk felt a little bad for the guy, but there was no other way. Sure, he could wait until Maria showed up, then tell her the bad

149

news and have a proper funeral, but then they may never know how to defeat the Head. If indeed the act of feeding Harman to it would give him any indication of weakness. Now that he thought about it . . . how *was* this going to help anything? He needed a body to get close to the Head, but that didn't mean he had to feed it. He rolled Harman over again and brushed the loose soil from his eyes.

"Please don't do that again. All I was saying-"

"Say I was to leave you here and tell the others it ate you, I'd need something in return."

"Yes! Anything! I can't do much in my current condition, but you can do anything you want with my body. I'll tell you anything you want to know. I'll . . . I'll . . ."

Henk looked around to make sure the others hadn't been tempted to take a peek and were currently watching them. When he was confident they were alone, he said: "I need to know everything you know about the Head."

Harman's eye's rolled back into the back of his skull before reappearing a moment later. "Well, uh. I don't know what I can say that you don't know already but . . . it's always been here. It started as a baby head and has been growing steadily over the years."

"Come on, Harman. I'm going to need more than that. What else?"

"Umm," Harman was starting to panic, knowing there was still plenty of time for Henk to change his mind again. "The Gimp feeds the dead to the Head, which seems to keep it happy. The Head has the power to summon killers into our

150

world—several of which you've dealt with personally. Some people believe it gets energy from eating the corpses. Grows more powerful. Others believe it's protecting our town from things far worse."

"What do *you* believe?"

"I believe there's a delicate balance between Sorrow and the Head. Although I agree it *does* need to feed, I don't think it has to be *every* corpse, the way it has been in recent years. My dad says they only used to feed it once every year or so back in his day."

It didn't seem as if Harman was aware of his father's fate, and Henk couldn't see anything good would come of telling him now. If indeed any of this *was* real, and he wasn't going to wake up in an institution at any minute. "Anything else?"

"No. Yes!" Harman panicked. "Everyone knows about it these days, even the tourists. Some of us think it's kind of quirky and don't mind it. Others cannot stand knowing it's out there somewhere. Maria is one of those that despises it, which is another reason she would be mortified if you fed me to it. She blames it for you and Dave leaving."

"What about the council?" Henk asked. He brushed his throat-leg aside as the wind picked up and blew it across his face. "They're the ones responsible for the decisions regarding feeding the Head. Who else is on it?"

"Well, my dad. Then there's Pastor Wicker . . . Matilda Henning . . . Billy Benderson . . . and Terrence Orpenhein."

"Three dead," Henk muttered. Did it mean anything? "Huh?"

"Nothing. Who's Orpenhein?"

"He's the mayor. Who's dead?"

Henk rubbed his chin—it was a warm afternoon, and he could feel sweat beginning to gather beneath his beard. "You are, buddy. Listen, I'm going to leave you here. I'll tell Maria where you are as long as you don't tell her any of what happened today, okay?"

It looked as if the corpse was trying to smile. "Good one."

Henk reached out and closed Harman's eyes, then stood and turned towards the bushes, to where a dazzling blue outline filled most of his vision. The head had indeed grown over the years. It was now at least twice the size it had been when he first saw it. Because the bushes were presenting as a shifting wall of hyena heads, and because he wanted to get a look at the thing without it appearing as a giant blue blob, Henk peeled the latex back from his face and let it fall behind his shoulders.

He could hear it breathing.

Shallow, shuddering breaths that stole the air from all around him. He felt lightheaded, which only worsened as he parted the leaves and the otherworldly smell hit him, like a box of rotten eggs that had passed through the intestinal tract of an entire city.

Henk fought the impulse to put the mask back on, to nullify the scent. His fingertips breached the opposite side of the shrubs, slowly parted them.

It was at least twice the size it had been when he last saw it. Heavy-lidded (sleeping?), rolling white eyes the size of basket balls. A flat, narrow nose, ended in a little rounded tip,

152

separating the pink, peach-fuzzed cheeks, which expanded with each breath drawn through its thin mouth. Its ears were sunken pits, stiff bristles of wax-coated hairs protruding in every direction. Henk watched the Head for a moment, wondering how on earth such a thing could exist in the first place. As far as he was aware, there had only ever been one attempt at destroying it, which had ended in the slaughter of the entire town. The attackers had opted to fire upon the entity from a distance, using a variety of rifles and other projectiles. According to those that discovered the massacre, the Head had sustained no visible damage.

Henk took a tentative step forward, his face at the edge of the clearing. What was he hoping for, exactly? It was just a head, aside from its unusual size and appetite. He took another step closer, the mo-gro in his bloodstream giving him the confidence he otherwise may not have had. Then, another. Before he knew it, he was standing in front of the creature, within reaching distance. Close enough to see the individual pores, the cracks around its lips, the ants, beetles, and millipedes that scuttled across its still features.

Aside from the Gimp, had anyone ever been this close to the Head before? No one that had lived to tell the tale. Henk felt a sudden rage towards the disgusting being that had not only ruined his childhood but also altered the entire course of his life. Without thinking, his fist was sailing towards the bridge of its nose.

WHOOM!

Henk was reeling through the air. Fields of green rushed by beneath him, wind burning his eyes and reducing his vision to a blur. He shut them, anticipating a hard landing that never came. Instead, he felt himself slowing gradually as if caught in a net, tightening, smothering him, and then . . .

POP!

He was on his feet, surrounded by total darkness. No, that was not entirely true; there was a line of pale light in the near distance. Miniature figures, arms waving as they conversed around a large oval table.

"We cannot proceed without knowing the potential dangers!" urged a slender woman. As the scene drew closer, Henk saw none other than Matilda Henning, his old teacher. Also present were Jeff Notabaddie, Pastor Wicker, Billy Benderson and an obese man with long wavy hair that he didn't recognise. If this was a meeting of Sorrow council, as it appeared to be, it was fair to assume the man was Terrence Orpenhein, the town mayor.

Orpenhein straightened in his chair, the edge of the table digging a deep trench across his bloated gut. "I'm afraid I must disagree. I possess one thing that the rest of you do not—an outsider's perspective. People *love* Sorrow and its sordid history, but the Head alone just isn't cutting it anymore. Visitor numbers have been falling quarterly. They're not interested in looking at static displays and models of long-gone people anymore. What they're looking for after making the journey down here is an *experience.*

Pastor Wicker pointed at Orpenhein across the table. "You would put the rest of us in danger to make a quick buck! And what will you do when visitors start to go missing? Or bodies are found? Do you not think that would drive people away?"

"He's not thought this through," Benderson said, slumping back in his chair and shaking his head. "I might have let a lot slide for the good of the town, but what you're asking here . . . it could land me in a whole heap of trouble."

"You would be kept out of the picture," Orpenhein said dismissively. "Simply look the other way when the reports start trickling in. We could even write a clause into our advertisements stating that the town would not be liable. People would see it as all part of the show, but if it ever came down to it, it would have us covered."

"I'm failing to see the part where this benefits the rest of us." Jeff Notabaddie straightened, "It wouldn't surprise me if you skip town once your pockets are lined, leaving us to deal with the fallout."

Orpenhein glared at the farmer. "How dare you. I may not have grown up in Sorrow like the rest of you, but how could you even consider that, after everything I've done for this town? When I happened upon this place, I saw a struggling economy on its last legs, citizens going through life on autopilot, depressed and unable to see a future. What I am proposing will not only line my own pockets, but the pockets of every resident in this town, yourselves included." Then, as he could tell the others were beginning to consider his proposition, "It's win-win for everyone."

155

There were several murmurings around the table. Henk was now standing alongside Matilda Henning, waving a hand in front of her face. His initial curiosity was starting to fade—where exactly was he? And what if he was stuck in this place forever?

Benderson finally spoke up: "As long as we make sure we're covered from a legal perspective . . ."

"That's beside the point," Wicker said. "We would never be covered in the eyes of God. Just because it's legal doesn't mean it's morally right."

"Can it, Wicker," Notabaddie muttered, "there *is* no God in Sorrow."

"Shall we take a vote, then?" Orpenhein asked. "All those in favour of feeding the Head, raise your hand." A smile crept across his face as hands began to rise around the table.

Realising he was outvoted four to one, Pastor Wicker curled his upper lip and raised his hand. "I want a new confessional booth."

"That'll be the first thing we get when the big money starts to roll in," Orpenhein said.

"And I want a new tractor," Notabaddie said.

Orpenhein nodded. "We're *all* going to benefit from this, and not only us, but the rest of the town, too. The seven wonders of the world *combined* haven't got shit on what we've got in our little town. It's only right we should be capitalising on it."

"Agreed," Henning said.

"It's decided then. As we all know, the Head will not be approached by anyone but the Gimp. Given that the Gimp has been dead for many years, we will require a volunteer to don the suit and feed the bodies of any future deceased to the head. Benderson, do you think this is something your boy could be persuaded to do?"

Benderson chuckled. "That boy's a filthy little pervert. He'd be pissed if I *didn't* ask him."

"Good. Then let us proceed with the plan. Remember, this is for the benefit of everyone. We can always stop if it ever gets out of hand. Or grows too big. Meeting adjourned."

The instant Orpenhein's open palm came down on the table, Henk awoke to Dave and Brett's worried faces looming over him. "Henk, are you okay, man?!" Dave said, his face-fingers reaching out for him. "Your eyes were rolling like a slot machine!"

Henk blinked several times and asked for space as he sat up and got his bearings. It took him a moment to remember what had happened, but when he did—

"Christ on a cum sock! What the hell?" Brett clasped both hands to his chin, grabbing at the red mark left behind by Henk's fist.

"You fucking asshole," Henk started. "You've been helping them the entire time."

Henk lunged for Brett once again, but Dave stepped in the way and held him back. "Woah, man. You were out of it. What are you talking about?"

Brett glowered at Henk but didn't say anything, waiting to hear what he had to say.

"I wasn't out of it," Henk said, still trying to push past his brother. "It showed me. The council are the reason for the spate of deaths. They've been feeding it, well, getting the fucking Knob Goblin to feed it, knowing it will only make it more powerful."

"Dude, listen to yourself for a minute," Dave said.

"No, you listen to me. I don't know how, but I was there. It was clear as day. They've been forcing the Head to grow. The more active it is, the more visitors come. More visitors mean more profit for them."

Brett held both hands out as Dave turned to face him. "I swear, you guys. I had no idea about any of this. They told me it had to eat to keep it happy, docile! As an officer of the law, it is my duty to protect the citizens of Sorrow with my life."

Dave pushed Henk back a little further before cautiously releasing him. "I believe him."

Henk lowered his head. "Sorry for hitting you, but you can see how it looks."

"Don't worry about it," Brett said, unwilling to look at him.

Henk peeled himself out of the gimp suit and tossed it back to him. "Put that somewhere safe. Somewhere your father can't find it."

They returned to the main road. "Wait," Dave said, looking anxiously at the fields, "what about Harman? You didn't . . .?"

"No. Fortunately, I wasn't able to before I got attacked, or whatever the hell that was."

"We should probably go and get the body then, right? I mean, we can't just leave him out here."

"No," Brett said. "It'll be safer there than anywhere else right now. If we take it in, there's a good chance someone else may try and feed it to the Head." He tossed the gimp suit in the boot of the driver's idling vehicle. "Besides, whoever killed him is still out there. Right now, our priority should be talking to Officer Benderson and seeing what he can tell us. As a member of the council, I'm afraid he's partially responsible for Jeff's death. Do you think you can deal with this, Brett?"

Brett nodded solemnly.

"All aboard the mystery express," Dave said, claiming the shotgun seat.

Henk hopped in the back alongside the Knob Goblin, unable to shake the thought that they could just as easily call the whole thing off and skip town again, return to his normal, boring life in the city. But there was still one thing preventing him from doing so. One thing he wasn't willing to leave unresolved a second time.

Maria.

Chapter 17

"No. No, no, no. This cannot be happening." Brett pushed through the ruined door of the police station and charged inside. The brothers followed at a safe distance. The otherworldly experience had sobered him up drastically, and only now did he realise quite how repulsive Dave looked with an extra arm, nose, and face-fingers.

Visibility inside was worse than ever. Thick smoke clogged their eyes. Smoke that became paste in their mouths. It was dust.

"Ever get the feeling you know what you're about to see before it happens?" Dave asked.

He was not wrong. Gone was the tissue-strewn floor of the police station. In its place was a sunken pit, which Brett was cautiously descending while calling his father's name. Henk was tempted to leave him to it, to wait outside in the fresh air, but he couldn't leave Brett to deal with this on his own. Not that he'd feel too guilty if anything were to happen to him (especially after everything he'd just learned), but because no matter how much he didn't want to, he *had* to see it for himself.

They followed Brett down the hole and into a cavern that stank of fresh earth. As expected, neon-blue fingers crisscrossed along the walls and guided them directly to the man at the middle of it all.

Billy Benderson was barely recognisable. Several feet off the ground and pinned against the rough surface of the wall, his skin had a blue tinge where it had made contact with the fingers. Parts of flesh on his exposed forearms and hands had been stripped away, and his face and neck were littered with blistering holes through which saliva dripped.

"Dad, keep still," Brett said as he ran to him. He wrapped his hands around the nearest giant finger, presumably intending to rip it free of his father, but screamed in pain as the acid attacked his hands. If he were thinking a little clearer, perhaps he would not have made such a stupid mistake.

Henk looked around for anything that could be used as a weapon to fend off the tendrils but came up short. Still high on mo-gro, Dave's brain decided it was a good idea to pick up a large rock and throw it in Billy's direction. It collided with his forehead and appeared to knock him out. Brett was too busy screaming and trying to stop the burning of his hands to notice. A moment later, both the fingers, and Billy, were gone.

"They'll be fine. A little scarring, but you're not going to lose them," Henk said as he tied off the bandages.

"I'm going to send Orpenhein down if it's the last thing I do," Brett responded. Henk had since told them everything that had gone on at the meeting, word for word. "It's his fault my father is dead. Matilda, Wicker . . ."

"Technically, Wicker killed himself," Dave said over the lip of his beer. He leant against the police station's doorframe and took another sip of the warm beverage while admiring Henk's first aid skills.

"Only because he couldn't live with the guilt of what they'd done," Henk said. "And even if he hadn't, the fingers would have gotten him."

Dave tossed the empty into the pit beyond the doorframe. "True dat."

"Orpenhein is to blame, sure. But they all went along with it. If he's lying low at home, which he most likely is, then he could be in serious danger, too. We should prioritise getting to him. Then, hopefully, everything else will fall into place."

"Good. Fuck him," Brett grumbled. "He doesn't give two shits about this town. I say we let him burn."

"You're the only form of authority this town has right now," Henk said. Brett seemed to like that. "You're sworn to protect the people of Sorrow and bring those that deserve it to justice. Wouldn't it be better to know that he was rotting in prison?"

"Getting buggered by bigger boys," Dave added helpfully.

Brett stood and inspected his bandaged hands. "I suppose I owe my old man that much. Maybe we'll find Maria there, too."

"Orpenhein's?" Henk had no idea why they would find Maria at the home of a man-slug like Terrence Orpenhein, but he supposed it was about as likely as anywhere else.

"Well, yeah. Don't tell me you boys didn't know about that, either?"

"Dude," Dave said between fits of laughter, "Harman, and now Orpenhein. Yet *you've* never managed to score with her? Hilarious."

Henk almost couldn't believe it. Actually, he couldn't believe it *at all*. That she'd have even a brief affair, or that the entire town had since found out about it. Why would Maria lower herself to sleeping with someone like Orpenhein? Perhaps he didn't know her as well as he thought after all—to say her taste in men was questionable would be an understatement . . . which, now he thought about it, actually made a little more sense that she would have liked him.

"Yep," Brett continued, "I heard Harman only found out because he grew suspicious enough to check her phone. Pissed his old man off to no end, that did. Said Harman was a fool for not calling the wedding off."

"She must be losing her mind to sleep with someone like him," Henk agreed.

They rocked up to the main gate of Orpenhein Manor. As the largest residence in Sorrow, it even had its own private gardens and half-mile drive. It was unclear where the mayor had come from before he'd arrived in town, but one thing was evident— he was doing just fine financially.

"Can I help you?" came a bored voice through the electronic panel to the left of the gates.

"Officer Brett Benderson on official business to see Terrence Orpenhein. Open up, please."

"I'm sorry, Mr Benderson, but Mr Orpenhein isn't taking visitors at this time."

"Officer. It's Officer Benderson. And you open this gate up right now, or I'll arrest you for obstructing the course of justice."

The woman on the other end made a point of keeping hold of the 'speak' button while she released a drawn-out sigh. There was a single bleep, and the gates started to roll inward.

"Thank you, Ma'am." But the Ma'am was already gone.

As they followed the winding gravelled drive, Henk had to admit he was a little impressed with the Knob Goblin's ability to put his emotions aside and focus on the task at hand. His years in Sorrow had given him a stiff upper lip. "So, we're just going straight in and arresting him?"

"If only it were that simple," Brett said. "Aside from a lack of evidence to prove that Orpenhein is primarily to blame for the recent deaths, I'm not sure I could ever convince a jury that any of what was being presented to them wasn't complete and utter baloney."

Dave wiggled his eyebrow-fingers. "No one would believe anything we said about the Head."

"Not that part, you idiot," Brett snapped. "The Head is the *easiest* part to prove—half the world knows about it already!

I'm talking about Orpenhein knowingly putting people in danger in exchange for a little extra cash."

"Especially when people are dying in Sorrow often enough as it is," Henk agreed. "There's so much false information relating to the murderers that it's impossible to keep track of the truth sometimes."

"Indeed. Which is why I need to feel him out. If he knows I'm onto him, he might try and skip town." They reached the front door, and Brett knocked twice. "Let me do the talking. In fact," he raised his eyebrows at Dave, "you should wait out here. There's no way you're coming in like that." Dave didn't seem overly bothered as he stalked off into the grounds to the side of the house.

The door opened to a mousy brunette with piercing green eyes and a slightly crooked nose. "Mr Orpenhein is on a call at the moment. Please, follow me." She led the way through an overly extravagant entrance hall lined with gold-framed paintings and ornate sculptures of indecipherable objects. "May I ask what your visit is concerning, Officer?"

"No, you may not. I'd rather speak with Terrence directly."

Henk was again surprised by Brett's ability to put on a professional front. It brought a subtle smile to his face to know he could bring it all down with two words, *Knob Goblin,* should he want to.

The receptionist (if that even was her official role) took them through to a small lounge with a worn leather two-seater sofa and a few bookshelves. "Please, have a seat. The mayor will be with you shortly." She then left the room through the same door they'd entered. Henk approached the tall window to the left of the bookshelf, which looked out onto the grounds. Several rosebushes nestled a large aviary. Dave was pressed against the metal bars, passing a glowing sprig of mo-gro through to a scarlet macaw.

Another door opened to Henk's left, and a rotund man in a tight brown suit appeared. He said, in a voice that seeped sliminess, "Officer Benderson, a pleasure, I'm sure. Please, come on through to my office." Brett followed the man into the next room and took a seat in front of an oversized walnut desk. Orpenhein took a seat across, and only then seemed to notice Henk. "And who might this be?"

"Henk Wolfe," Henk said as he slid into the seat next to Brett.

"Cut the shit," Brett said. "You know who this is. Henk's friend is missing. We were hoping you might be able to help us out."

Orpenhein folded his pudgy hands across his gut. "Oh?"

"Maria Wendall," Brett continued. "I believe you know of her."

The mayor spread his hands wide. A hint of a smile dented his blotchy cheeks, "Come on now, Brett. What happened between us is all in the past, though I'm flattered that you think I might know where she is now."

Henk said: "Something is going on in this town, Mr Orpenhein, and I'm worried for her safety. We were hoping she might have had some kind of contact with you in the last couple of days?"

"Boys," Orpenhein started. For a moment, Henk thought he saw a glimmer of frustration behind the man's smile. "I haven't spoken to the girl since her and I . . . terminated our fling. I'm afraid I cannot help you."

"In that case," Brett said coolly, "let us move on to the other reason we're here. You should know that I believe you to be in immediate danger. Over the last forty-eight hours, every member of the Sorrow council has been murdered."

The mayor's eyes widened just enough to make it clear he'd been unaware of this development until now. "I'm sorry for your loss, Officer Benderson. May I ask how they . . ."

"The Head. The fingers took them all."

"Terrible," Orpenhein muttered. He reached into a small drawer at the front of his desk, removed an embroidered handkerchief and began blotting at his pitted forehead. "But why target the council? And why now? We've been living in relative peacetimes for years."

"That's what we're worried about," Brett said, leaning forward, "It's not happy about something, and I would like to know what. Now, I'll ask you again. Can you tell us anything that may help me in my investigation? Why might it be targeting the council in particular?"

Orpenhein rested his elbows on the table and let his face fall into his hands. After a moment, he shook his head and muttered: "Crazy bitch. Going to get us all killed." They waited patiently for the mayor to elaborate, worried that any interruption would cause him to stop talking. "She's lost it."

"Terrence," Brett said, "I need you to tell me what you know."

Orpenhein lifted his head. His eyes were glistening, threatening to burst. "We never slept together," he paused to dab his eyes with the handkerchief, "she made me send her text messages and pictures of myself to make her fiancé think we were having an affair. She wanted to discredit me. To cause a rift in the council."

"What?" Henk said, "And you just let her? Why would she do that?"

"She blames me for putting this town on the map. For bringing attention to the Head . . . all I ever wanted was what's best for Sorrow." Orpenhein took a deep breath, then stood up and went to the window, his back to the others. "When I came here, this town was on its last legs. But I saw the untapped *potential* that it held. Sorrow was all but deserted, its history leaving it tarred as a black spot on the map, a mistake that was waiting to be erased, but I reasoned that by playing *into* its . . . unique features, we could create a place that people would travel from all over the world to see."

"Well, you succeeded in one thing then," Henk said.

Orpenhein spun. "A vote was held, and although it ultimately passed, I failed to consider the lengths some of the residents would go to watch the town fade into obscurity."

Henk could understand where the 'residents' had been coming from—if he'd been living in Sorrow at the time, there was no doubt he would have been one of those that resisted the proposition.

"Regrettably," the mayor continued, "many of the remaining residents moved away after we started turning the place into a tourist attraction, unwilling to be involved, despite the potential for profit for everyone. Maria was one of the only ones that stayed behind, but even she was not happy with the changes. She made that *perfectly* clear on several occasions."

Brett cleared his throat. "So, she doesn't like you. That still doesn't explain how she persuaded you to send her sensitive photos." Orpenhein looked at Henk as if unwilling to divulge the information with a stranger present. "Henk grew up here," Brett confided, "he likely knows more about what's going on here than you do."

Orpenhein nodded, face flushed. "It really is you. A Son of Sorrow, right here in my office."

"Please," Henk said, "just tell us."

"She found out about the bodies . . . and the Gimp." He looked to Henk once again as if expecting him to ask what the hell he was talking about. When Henk didn't, he said: "She saw a body being transported for feeding one evening and followed you, Brett. Saw what we were doing with our dead. Got the crazy idea that we'd fed her parents to the Head after the accident and was threatening to go to the press with the story unless I helped her. I didn't ask why she wanted me to do it—it seemed like I was getting off lightly, in all honesty. Then, after Henning's house burnt down, she told me I was not to let her stay here. I didn't ask why, but I last heard she was staying in the old college."

"Well, did you?" Henk asked. "Feed her parents to the Head?"

"Of course not!" Orpenhein grunted. "They were far too burnt to be salvageable. The urn she received was real, although it was mostly burned timber with a few teeth in it." Then, on seeing Henk's disbelieving face, "What? It was all we could recover."

Brett relaxed back in his chair. "Let me get this straight. Maria comes to tell you she knows we've been feeding the Head bodies to make it grow. She says she wants to make it look as if the two of you are having an affair, causing distrust among two of the most influential members of the council, yourself and Jeff Notabaddie. I'm still failing to see what she hoped to get out of it. And why bring Harman into it?"

"Harman was only there because no one else would be. That much was clear. And how should I know what she was hoping to get out of it? She's lost the plot. All she cares about is ruining the good things we've spent years building for our town, watching it all come down."

"Oh, shit," Henk said, piecing it all together. "Henning's dead, too. We saw her in Two Trees." The other two looked to him expectantly, but he was still processing all this new information. Could she really be doing what he thought she was?

"It's all there," he said finally. "Maria's plan might not have gone exactly how she'd been expecting, but she was able to break down communication between the lot of you enough that you wouldn't know the danger until it was too late."

"Is Harman okay?" Orpenhein asked.

Ignoring him, Henk continued. "The false affair. Causing Harman's relationship with his father to break down. Henning's house burning. She's knows it's only a matter of time before the rift will open again, and you guys have been playing right into it."

"What makes you so sure all of a sudden?" Brett asked.

"How do you not see it yet? The Head has never directly been a danger. With each body fed to it, the chances of the rift reopening have been increasing. I don't think it *wants* to eat the dead. It's been trying to show us that by targeting those responsible for the decision. It never asked to be the circus attraction you've turned it into. It's all there in Wicker's book. I think Maria killed Harman and planned to drop him into the rift as a final offering. The sacrifice of a betrothed, but she killed him too early. We found his body and moved it, which means—"

"Wait, wait," Orpenhein said, starting to panic. "I'm still alive, and if you guys have already moved Harman, surely we're in the clear? All that's left is to find her and arrest her, right?" Orpenhein swept a clammy hand across his forehead as he looked between Brett and Henk. "It's not too late. RIGHT?"

Henk wished he could give a confident response to the sweaty man. He'd gone there ready for a fight but ended up feeling sorry for him, more than anything else. The mayor was simply another pawn in Maria's scheme, dragged along for the ride while kept under the impression he was still in control. "We need to bring Dave in," Henk said, rushing past the desk to the window.

171

MATTHEW A. CLARKE

A piercing scream came from upstairs.

Chapter 18

Case Sixteen: The Rift. March 9th, 2012

"It might sound a little strange, but I'm going to miss our little outings when we've dealt with it," Dave said, kicking a rock ahead of them.

"Outings?" Maria said, "Dave, we're doing this for a reason. You do understand that? It's not some game."

"Yeah . . . I know. I just kind of enjoy fighting the forces of evil, is all."

"Don't we know it," Henk said. "There's no guarantee this will even work, so you might be in luck."

It was true—they were dealing with the unknown in going after the Rift. There were no guarantees that any of them would be walking away from it, either, but the existence of such a thing sure explained a lot when it came to Sorrow's history.

The Sons of Sorrow had received a tip-off from a dog walker after she stumbled across a strange hole in the middle of the forest. At first, she told them, she thought it was just a large badger hole, one of many dotted about the area. But after Pinkypaws, her Chihuahua, entered the hole and failed to return, she'd been forced to take a closer look. Instead of a dark, musky tunnel, as she'd been expecting, she'd seen a swirling blue light instead. Pinkypaws had then re-emerged from the hole, and stood on his hind legs, proceeded to command his owner to get on all fours and put his leash on. The dog walker fled, sprinted to their clubhouse in Maria's parents' garden.

"Can I at least keep the dog once we're done?" Dave asked over his shoulder.

Henk wanted to tell him that if anything, the dog should be returned to its rightful owner once they'd sealed the Rift, but Maria said: "Sure, you can, Dave," before he had a chance. She tilted her head to one side and looked to Henk as if to say, *"Whatever makes him happy."*

"Shouldn't be far, now," Henk said. Then, pointing to a tree with a knot that looked like a bulbous nose, "That must be the tree she was talking about."

"Which meant Pinkypaws would have been . . ." Maria took a moment to gauge the angle, "this way."

"Ready?" Dave asked, pulling a bag of doggie treats and a laser pen from one of many Velcro pockets attached to his belt.

"Let's bag us a doggo, then sort this town out for good," Maria said.

Henk nodded in agreement but was still feeling a little uneasy about the whole situation. Sure, taking care of an entitled chihuahua shouldn't be too much of a problem, but what about the Rift? If it really was the source of the entities, as they suspected it to be, how were they going to go about sealing it? As he brushed aside spindly branches and overgrown weeds, he found himself wondering if they were out of their depth—what if the original settlers had attempted to do the very thing they were about to do and ended up getting the entire town slaughtered?

Henk had been so caught up in his thoughts he almost walked straight into Dave and Maria, who had paused a few steps ahead. "What is it?" he whispered.

Ahead was the biggest fucking chihuahua Henk had ever seen. It was bent on the floor in a large C, head nuzzling furiously at its groin. Bulging muscles rippled beneath its short, golden coat. Sharp, black claws sank deeper into the dirt as it forced its head lower. Behind the massive mutt was a wide hole in the earth.

"Who's a good boy?" Dave said, taking the lead. He stepped forward, a dog treat in each hand. Pinkypaws snapped his head away from his asshole to the sound of the human voice. His eyes pulsed ocean blue. "I love your eyes," Dave said, entirely unphased. "Good boy eyes."

The chihuahua stood on its hind legs, almost as tall as the humans, flexed its swollen pectorals, and cracked its paws. "Who you calling a good boy, bitch?" it said with a disturbingly deep voice.

"Woah. We come in peace," Maria said, stepping in. "With a body like that, you must need a lot of food. We have treats if you're willing to work with us."

"I've got a treat for *you*." Pinkypaws grabbed his groin. "How about we ditch these two dickheads, and I show you the *real* Pinkypaws."

Having remained on the side-lines up until now, Henk looked the dog directly in its mesmerising eyes. It snarled as if it knew what he was thinking, displaying a set of dino-grade teeth. "How about we give you two some alone time, Pinkypaws?"

"Call me that one more time. I fucking dare you."

Henk resisted the urge to run, knowing the muscle-clad dog could tear him to shreds if it decided to. Dave crouched and placed the bag of bone-shaped treats on the ground, then stepped away. "Take it easy, big guy. My brother and I will leave you two to get better acquainted. We'll be back in ten minutes and see if we can come to some kind of arrangement?"

"Better make it an hour," the dog said, already losing interest in the males. "I'm going to destroy this bitch."

"Guys, you can't just-" Maria started.

"On your knees," Pinkypaws commanded.

"Don't worry," Henk whispered from the corner of his mouth. He and Dave retreated slowly away from the scene as Maria dropped to her knees with a slack jaw. He heard the dog bark another order, then watched as Maria started to crawl toward it.

"Shit. We'd better hurry, or there's going to be nothing we can do to stop that thing from pounding her," Dave said.

Henk's penis twinged for reasons he decided were better left alone. He told himself it was just the thought of Maria getting pounded by *anything* that was a turn-on, not because it was a mutant dog with a cock the size of his forearm.

They broke the line of sight then immediately circled back around to the side, keeping low as they passed areas with little cover until eventually, they had eyes on them once more. The beast was standing behind Maria, still on her knees, facing away from it. Pinkypaws spat onto his paw, stroked his slick red snake, readying himself for entry. Maria covered her head as the dog howled, wiped the excess saliva on his shiny coat, and with his free paw, dug his claws under the waist of her jeans. After spending a moment trying to tug them down, he gave up and used his index claw to tear a large hole in the fabric between her legs.

The chihuahua's member pulsed as he dropped to his haunches and bent it so the tip was aligned with the rip in Maria's trousers. "Tell me I'm a good boy," he growled. Pinkypaws was too distracted to notice Dave creeping up behind him.

The demon dog yapped as Dave lashed out with a bowie knife, severing his member at the base with a clean downward slash. The shiny meat shot several feet along the ground in a wild spurt of crimson before sputtering to a stop.

Pinkypaws flailed, caught Dave in the face with the back of his meaty paw and sent several teeth down the back of his throat. Dave fell backwards, coughing and grasping at his neck. Maria performed a sprinter's start, putting distance between herself and the would-be rapist while Henk swung a log at its face. Pinkypaws dropped like a sack of burning dogshit, his snout twisted along the side of his face, one eye ruptured and pissing white fluid. He remained down, yelping and trying to stem the blood flow between his legs.

A moment later, he fell unconscious.

"Took you long enough," Maria shouted as she ran over to clear Dave's airway.

Henk tossed the log to the ground. "We wouldn't have let him put it in you."

177

"Well, you certainly had the two of us believing otherwise."

Dave puked a handful of teeth after Maria's open palm connected with his back for the third time. She then stood and reached around to check the hole in her jeans. No blood, at least. "Is it dead?"

"I'm not sure," Henk replied. "If not, it will be soon. There's more gore than a bomb at a blood drive."

Dave was back on his feet, prodding the splintered prongs in his gums. "Yough welcam," he said to Maria.

"Sorry. I didn't mean to sound ungrateful before. And I'm sorry about your teeth."

"It okah. I grow moar."

"Sure you will, buddy," Henk said.

They moved past the furry freak and approached the hole it had been guarding.

"So, *this* is the Rift, huh?" Maria mused. "I kinda expected it to be a little more impressive."

The others agreed. It was almost a perfect circle, perhaps a little more than shoulder-width. The bright neon light at the bottom was almost entirely hidden beneath the swirling blue mist that rose from it. (Even more peculiar: the fog was evaporating before it could leave the hole).

"Smell 'ike 'ubble-gum," Dave said, smiling through bloodied gums.

"Don't try to taste it," Henk warned, just in case.

Maria started stroking her cheeks. "So, how are we doing this? Fill it in with soil? Hit it with sticks? Stuff Pinkypaws back down there?"

178

"I guess we try all of the above," Henk said.

None of the above worked. Whatever they put into the hole simply vanished without a trace, evaporated. They spent several hours circling, trying and failing to close the Rift until they started losing daylight.

"We can't just leave it. What if something else comes through tonight and kills someone? It'll be on our heads." Maria peered over the edge once again. "I've got an idea. Take your shirts off. Both of you."

Henk and Dave shared a wink. Maria rolled her eyes.

"Now stand here. No," she moved them into position by their shoulders, "here. And use them to try and fan the hole."

Once they'd got the hang of wafting in tandem, they were able to get a decent rhythm going and soon cleared enough of the luminous mist to see beyond it.

"Is that . . ."

"An egg," Henk said between swings.

A few metres below ground level, nestled within a mess of pulsing fingers, was a blue egg-shaped object the size of a toddler. Its surface was covered in a sinewy membrane. Now and then, it would appear to wiggle slightly, and a fresh puff of fog would spew from the fingers connected to it. "That must be what's powering it."

"I geth," Dave said. "Wha 'ow?"

"Keep doing what you're doing," Maria said, "I'll be back in a second."

Maria returned with the log covered in Pinkypaws's clotting blood. After waiting a moment to see if anyone would object,

179

she held it over the egg-shaped object like a mining drill, then brought it down.

Henk braced. He'd been expecting something catastrophic to happen the second the log connected, but it simply popped the supple jelly-like substance into the three-foot fingers beneath. There was a whining shriek from all around them as the fingers tore themselves from their coil, stiffened, and shot straight out of the orifice as high as the surrounding trees. Then, they retracted, taking the remains of the egg with them.

Henk slid his t-shirt back over his head. "Is that it? Did we do it?"

Maria clucked her tongue. "It appears so."

"Tuh same fingeth," Dave offered.

"Yeah. Whatever the 'Rift' was, it was either feeding off or being fed *by* the fingers. And the fingers looked exactly like the ones I saw wrapped around the Head."

"Which means the Head and the fingers are connected?" Maria asked as if expecting him to know the answer.

"I do not know the answer," Henk said, "and I don't think we ever will, but the Rift is gone, and that's all that matters."

They stood around the empty pit for several moments in comfortable silence, realising they'd come to the end of an era. Henk was unsure how to feel about this. The town was safer than it'd ever been thanks to them, but his parents were still dead, as the other kids at the orphanage would remind him almost daily (not that theirs were any more alive). Fighting crime had been the one thing that was able to take his mind away from his shitty reality, but they'd just ensured that chapter of their lives was over.

Looking at Maria, he wondered if she was thinking the same thing. His arm spasmed as if urging him to slip it around her waist and pull her body against his own. She was looking at him funny. He realised he was staring.

Now or never.

"EYY!" Dave screamed, spraying gummy phlegm into Henk's face. "Chech it ouh! Space buhd!" He threw himself to the earth, plucked a sprig of luminous bud from the wall of the pit and held it under his nostrils. "Smelth awethome. Bet it giveth superpowerth or somethith!"

The moment was gone.

Perhaps forever.

Chapter 19

Orpenhein was surprisingly fast for a big guy. His gut collided with the table as he bolted for the door, knocking it across the natural wood flooring and onto the laps of the other two.

"WAIT!" Henk shouted, struggling to free his legs, but the mayor was a man possessed. He barrelled through to the entrance hall and mounted the stairs faster than the others could keep up. Henk took two steps at a time and found himself in a red-carpeted hallway that branched off in either direction with no indication as to which way Orpenhein had gone.

Another scream, followed quickly by a dull thud.

Henk ran left, ignoring the doors passing by as he followed the sounds of a struggle. The hall ended in a heavy oak door, which, although partially open, slammed as he reached it, knocking him back. He checked Brett was still close before twisting the brass handle and forcing his way inside.

Orpenhein was on the floor inside the doorway, groaning and holding his head. Across from him, standing in front of the bay window of the regal bedroom, was a hulk of a figure. Her coin-sock breasts were crammed into a tight, red spandex suit, forced sideways beneath her armpits, and a red hood was pulled low over her (presumably) grotesque features. "Tormentor," Henk muttered.

Tilly the Tormentor curtseyed before bending to wrap a sausage hand around the back of the receptionist's head. From the way her limbs were positioned beneath her, Henk had thought her dead, but she uttered an unnerving moan as she was lifted without any sign of strain from the aggressor. The Tormentor spun on her heel and smashed the receptionist's face through the double-glazed glass in one fluid motion, dragging her throat along the blades stuck in the bottom of the frame.

Fingers, fat and thin, immediately began worming their way through the window, over the spasming corpse and along the walls towards the mayor.

"No!" Orpenhein cried, attempting to stand but still rocked from the blow to his head; he fell to his knees while trying to charge the Tormentor.

"Grab him," Brett said, pushing past Henk to grab a fistful of the mayor's waistcoat. He was able to drag him back a few inches before the Tormentor lifted the receptionist's body over her head and hurled it at them. The mayor squealed like a pig as the body wrapped around the dresser beside him. Henk and Brett took a wrist each and were able to pull the blubbering man out into the hallway before he became stuck. Several thin fingers and one considerably chubby one had latched onto Orpenhein's shoes and wound their way up his legs. He screamed in agony as they released their digesting enzymes, and the smell of burning meat was diffused with the help of the breeze from the open window.

"Friggin' fingies," Henk said. "Pull harder!"

They dropped to the floor as the opposing force strengthened, kicking away with their feet as they desperately fought for purchase on the thick pile carpet. Meanwhile,

Orpenhein was screaming for his life and generally not contributing to the situation in any constructive way. There was a sickening tearing sound as the meat of his legs slid away from his body as if his bones had been wearing them as fleshy sheaths.

The others used the momentary slack to their advantage and resumed pulling, leaving a thick wet smear along the red carpet. They made it as far as the staircase before Tilly the Tormentor caught up to them. Forced to release Orpenhein, Henk raised his fists in preparation for what he expected to be a fairly quick fight (and the end of his life).

But it wasn't Henk that Tilly the Tormentor had in her sights when she charged. His fist bounced off a shoulder of steel as the hooded woman trampled over Orpenhein and clotheslined the Knob Goblin over the bannister. "NO!" Henk cried. No matter how hard he shoved the back of her broad shoulders, he could not budge her. Tiring of his flea-like pestering, she turned to him, spread her arms wide for a crushing blow.

Henk ducked, and the oversized hands clapped together right where his head would have been.

"It burns," Orpenhein wept.

The fingers were back, working their way up his waist to his chest and throat, but Henk was powerless to help the fat man. One misstep, and he would be dead, too. He let his instincts take over, watched as his legs carried him down the stairs at breakneck speed, skirting Brett's unmoving shape on his way out the front door.

Henk regained control of his body after staggering down the front steps and onto the winding path to the main gate.

"Dave?" Henk yelled. "We need to get out of here!" The top-left side of the mayor's mansion exploded outward in a firework of brick and mortar as the Tormentor charged through the first floor. Henk watched as Dave appeared from the direction of the aviary, right in the path of the meat missile. "DAVE!" he screamed, but it was too late to do anything but watch. Fortunately, Dave tripped over an errant brick and stumbled out of her way at the last second. In Dave's wake, Tilly the Tormentor was swarmed by a pandemonium of multi-beaked recently-released parrots. Protecting their saviour, they reduced the mass of meat to a sputtering nub within seconds.

The brothers were halfway down the path to the main road when the first blood-chilling child-like screams filled the air.

Small bodies littered the streets.

Bodies of children left to fend for themselves when the entities swarmed the town. Here and there were larger limbs, a split head, or a shredded groin, but the easiest targets had been the kids.

"*Over here,*" urged a female voice.

A small woman with a strip of flesh missing below her left eye was motioning for them from the doorway of a souvenir shop. "Where is everyone?" Henk asked after she shut them inside.

"Dead. Probably. I don't know. I was lucky enough to have three kids. I told them to go and ask the Square Boi Slasher for an autograph and was able to dive in here while he was busy taking care of them. Did you see him? The Square Boi? Is he gone?"

"Not sure," Dave said, his face still a writhing blanket of fingers. "Is that why people are bringing their kids here? In case shit goes south?"

The woman wrinkled her nose. "Why the hell else would I bring children here?"

Henk pulled Dave to one side. "I think Maria has done it. She's reopened the Rift. With the Head as big as it is now, I'm betting the Rift has got so much power it doesn't know what to do with itself."

"But . . . Maria?"

"Keep up. Orpenhein and Brett dead. Maria bad. She crazy. Pissed at the town or at me or whatever it is this time." Henk only heard the statement after it left his mouth, realised it was probably saying things like that which cemented his single status.

"Yes, we all know women are impossible to understand," Dave agreed, "but what are we going to do about it?"

The woman scowled at the pair, but if they were point-scoring, she was already way in the lead for sacrificing her muff mites.

"We're going to close it. Again. And if Maria is responsible for this, we're going to fuck her up, too."

"Yeah!"

"This conversation doesn't include you," Henk said to the woman.

Although it was impossible to get a decent read on how Dave was feeling about it through facial features, his tilted posture said he was uncertain. Finally, he said, "I don't think Maria would do this. She loved kicking monster butt almost as much as I do. There's no way she'd help them."

"People change. All I'm saying is *if* she's responsible, she's in trouble, okay?"

"Sounds fair to me," Dave shrugged.

Henk knew there was only one thing that would get his brother in the mood for the task ahead. He held his hand out in front of him, palm down. "Sons of Sorrow."

Dave stared at the hand for a moment before a smile cracked across his face. "You son of a bitch, I'm in." He slapped his hand over Henk's. On three, they threw their hands up to the ceiling. "Sons of Sorrow!"

"Sorry to break up your little moment," said the woman with dead kids, "but we appear to have company."

Standing across the street, clutching a child's spinal column at waist height (skull still attached), was Cornelius Square, AKA the Square Boi Slasher. The Square Boi was known for mutilating anyone unable to answer a complex mathematical question on the spot. The last time they'd dealt with him, the Sons of Sorrow discovered his only weakness, the most complex equation he'd been presented with—how to solve the irreparable damage caused by an axe blow to the face.

Dave snatched a glass paperweight with Henk's face on it from a shelf near the counter, then kicked the front door open. "I thought we killed your ugly ass already?"

The Square Boi sneered, adjusted his inch-thick glasses, which rested awkwardly across a raised welt of pink scar tissue where his nose should have been.

"I'm not sure attracting his attention was a good idea," Henk said. "We're unarmed."

"What do you mean? We've got weapons all around us!" As if to prove his point, Dave hurled the paperweight at the Square Boi's face.

The Square Boi side-stepped it easily, and holding the child's vertebral column as a bat, smashed the projectile back at them, cracking both the skull and the gift shop window as the paperweight hit it dead centre.

"Get behind me!" the woman screamed somewhat unexpectantly. Muttering barely audibly: "Didn't want it to come to this so soon, but needs must."

"Wait. What are you doing?" Henk asked as the woman produced a swaddled baby from behind a stack of 'Spooky Sorrow' hoodies.

"It's the only way."

"Fuck that," Dave said as the Square Boi began skulking across the street towards them. "We can take him. Right, Henk?"

The little pink hat slipped off the baby's head. It began to cry.

"See? She knows this is her destiny. Shhh. You'll be with your brother and sister soon."

Dave ducked the little spinal column as it whistled a morbid melody through the air and embedded itself in a cork notice board on the wall behind him. The woman used the moment to slip past and rush out the front door with her baby outstretched.

"Please. A gift. Just let me go."

The Square Boi drove his forehead into the woman's face, shattering her nose and producing dual black eyes. As she dropped to her knees, clutching at her ruined face, the Square Boi caught the baby by its legs and used it to club the woman's skull repeatedly.

Henk and Dave slipped out the back door and into the narrow alleyway at the rear of the store. "Oh man, we're so *fucked,*" Dave panted.

Henk slapped him about the face once, twice. Then once again.

"Thanks," Dave said as blood trickled from his left nostril. "I needed that."

"We're not dying here. All we need to do is get back to the rift and stop Maria."

Dave ran his hands through his finger-face, sweat beading along his hairline.

189

Henk slapped his brother once more. "The Head's more powerful than ever. There's no telling what might come through if we don't stop it."

Dave wiped the blood from the corner of his mouth with the back of his hand, "Let me get this straight. You're suggesting we try to get all the way across town to a place where the Rift may or may not even be, to stop something that may or may not be trying to come through to our world while potentially killing our childhood friend?"

"Pretty much."

"Right. Well, we're not going to get very far without weapons, and I'm not seeing any kids around . . ."

"Jenk's place is down this way," Henk gestured to the opposite end of the alley. "Maybe he can help us."

Dave didn't need any convincing—the sound of demolition coming from inside the souvenir shop was enough. They hustled down the alley and across the street. A short run to the right was Jenk's. It was more of a hoarder's paradise than anything else, with random junk piled high against the walls and windows. After checking the street was clear of immediate danger, they made their move. Dave bounced straight off the door and landed on his rump in the gutter, while Henk pulled the door the correct way and held it open until his brother had collected himself.

The place stank of dust and cat piss (which was odd, given the volume of rats that ran for cover). "Anyone home?" Henk called. He nudged a stack of warped DVD cases with the tip of his boot, setting off a small avalanche.

"There's no way Jenk made it," Dave said. "Let's just see if we can find anything useful and get out of here."

A metallic rustling came from beyond a mountain of comic books towards the back of the store. "Think again, bucko."

Jenk had somehow bent his car into a custom-made suit of armour, broken down and fused to his flesh, encompassing his massive stature. A large saucepan was crammed on top of his head. He held a broadsword in one hand and a sharpened length of metal in the other. Jenk waddled into the middle of the room, a smug look across his shapeless face. "I don't know what's going on around here, but I'll be damned if I'm not ready for it."

"Any chance you've got a couple of those suits going spare?" Dave asked.

Jenk's jowls flapped as he shook his head. "Sorry, boys. Took every inch of that car to make my own. Plenty of blades to go around, though." He offered the length of sharpened metal to Henk and the sword to Dave. Then, he shuffled back to the rear of the store and returned with a set of Ninja Sai daggers (which looked more like toothpicks in his bloated hands). "Any idea how many of these bastards we've got to put in the ground?"

After filling Jenk in on the situation, they managed to formulate some semblance of a plan. Jenk would carve a path across the town toward the woods, while the other two stayed behind him and his suit of armour wherever possible. Simple, yet—hopefully—effective.

Stealth was impossible, given the amount of noise the shrieking metal suit made as they started down the street outside, skirting shredded corpses. If anything, Henk thought, Jenk may be attracting more attention than they otherwise would've.

A child's cry emanated from the bakery off to their left. They passed as quickly as possible but were unable to get away without the assailant noticing them. "Going somewhere?" asked a weak voice.

"Sweet Choco Macchiato," Jenk said, his eyes narrowing beneath the saucepan. Then, to Henk, "How is that kid still alive?"

"The Puppeteer," Dave muttered.

The dead boy stood outside the bakery bowed, fresh blood from the gash at his throat falling to the pavement. He was missing an arm, but that didn't slow him at all as he skipped into the road. After a fancy flourish, the boy pointed a metal dough thermometer in their direction.

Henk nudged Jenk from behind, pointed to the near-translucent threads trailing from the back of the boy's joints. "There. You see?" Without waiting for a response, he said, "Keep him occupied. We'll try and get the jump on the Puppeteer."

192

"Or I could just do this." Jenk waddled toward the child. The dead kid's paltry weapon skimmed off his armour, nothing he could do to stop Jenk from bellyflopping onto him. There was a wet squelch, and a spurt of rouge shot from beneath the metal suit in all directions

"I guess that works too," Henk said. Dave rolled the big man over to the nearest lamp post so he could pull himself back to his feet. The front of Jenk's armour was dripping with gore.

"That wasn't too friendly," said another dead child, this one a petite girl with her lower jaw split in the middle. She charged the trio, screaming, with a lit blowtorch outstretched. Jenks lashed out with a ninja dagger, but the girl shifted to the side and leapt onto the front of his suit, thrusting the lit mouth of the blowtorch at his face. Jenk screamed as his left eye bubbled, gunk exploding down his cheek. The girl switched onto the other while he thrust wildly with both blades. His attacks did nothing to slow her. Panicking, he dropped the daggers and flailed, blind, knocking both Henk and Dave aside as they rushed in to help. The girl cackled as she moved the blue flame to the saucepan atop Jenk's head, heating the meaty contents.

Henk gathered himself in time to see Dave swinging the heavy sword in a wide horizontal arc. The blade separated the girl just above the waist and shook violently in his hands as it followed through to Jenks's armour. Both the girl and the still-lit blowtorch hit the ground, the open flame catching her hair and turning her screaming head into a fireball, but the damage to Jenk had already been done.

The big man wailed, pawing at his ruined face, an uneven mess of blackened flesh and weeping, open sores. He tripped over the dead girl's upper half and face-planted the ground with an earth-shaking impact. Henk moved to help, lifted Jenk's head, saw he'd landed on top of one of his three-pronged daggers, the hilt protruding from between his lips, angled upward through the top of his head. He supposed it was a mercy given what he'd been going through. "We should get out of here before more show up."

Dave nodded without taking his eyes off the entrance of the bakery. It was unlikely the Puppetter was inside—he could be hiding in any one of the nearby buildings. It would be safer to keep moving instead of searching for a fight. Before they set off, however: "Give me a hand with this." He grabbed the roof panel strapped to Jenk's back and started peeling away the metal banding. Henk loosened a second length of metal, relinquishing the car's bonnet from the big man's buttocks. Moments later, they were both armed with a blade and a shield.

They'd almost made it to the end of the road when two more dead kids rose from the gutters and charged them. Henk wasn't sure he had it in him to butcher a child (regardless of whether they identified as alive) but found he didn't feel bad at all about cutting the little boy's head off his neck after he'd tried to bite him on the leg. He slammed the kid's headless body to the floor with a quick smash of his shield.

"RUN!" screamed a male voice. Moments later, a young man in gym shorts and a vest top came tearing around the corner, wide flaps of skin trailing uselessly from either arm. "WHERE

194

ARE ALL THE CHILDREN?" he screamed, flipping the nearest corpse and screaming into the dead girl's face, "WE NEED MORE CHILDREN." He stiffened, then collapsed to reveal the Square Boi behind him, brandishing a jagged metal blade of his own.

"He must have followed us into Jenk's," Henk said, taking a wide stance. Dave followed suit. Shields raised, they took a step towards the Square Boi.

The Square Boi matched them pace for pace until the opposing forces were within striking distance, each waiting for the other to make the first move. Ten minutes later, Square Boi thrust the jagged metal at Henk, keeping his other hand behind him, out of harm's way.

Henk parried it effortlessly and countered with a stab of his own, puncturing the Square Boi in the abdomen. Unphased by the penetration, the Square Boi continued attacking, stabbing wildly. Metal screeched against metal as each attack was deflected. Still, the freak continued his relentless frenzy until, eventually, his blade slipped at an awkward angle and severed several of his own fingers.

Dave was on the Square Boi before he had a chance to snatch the weapon from the floor with his good hand, choosing to ditch the shield and put all of his weight behind a downward strike with the broadsword. The blade divided the left side of his torso from the right, subtracting organs.

"Damn, son," Henk said. "That was some medieval shit right there."

Dave smirked and collected his shield.

"WATCH OUT!" Henk screamed, spotting the silky string in the reflection of Dave's shield as it went for the back of his head. Instead, it passed over his shoulder and latched onto Dave's sword, whipping it away faster than either of them could react. Another thread lowered itself from the skies and stole Henk's shield. "In there!"

Ducking and weaving the errant threads, they charged into the nearest building, only to be greeted by a wooden snickering from all around. "Nope," Henk said. He went back for the doors but found they were already blocked; countless threads had woven around the handles. He tugged twice before coming to terms with the fact they would not be getting out the same way they came in.

"I'm tired of this asshole," Dave said.

With a sigh, Henk said, "He's not going to let us go until we've dealt with him."

They were standing in the reception area of some type of cosmetic clinic. They moved from room to room as quietly as possible, freezing each time they heard the disembodied giggling. Each room was similar in size and layout in that it had one adjustable bed similar to a dentist's and a row of white cupboards and shelving wrapped around three of the walls. There were charts of misshapen breasts in some rooms and photographs of caved noses in others. Upon peering into the sixth of such spaces, they came across a young woman in a white coat cowering by the cabinets, her upper half stuffed into the clearly-too-small cupboard as if she'd been trying to hide.

"Have you seen a skinny guy with a creepy nose around here?" Henk asked.

The woman didn't respond.

"You know we can see you, right?" Dave said. "Hey, lady?"

Henk approached the woman and placed a hand on the middle of her back. She slid out, twisted awkwardly and landed face-up on the floor. Or should that have been ears-up? The woman's face had been mixed up—her nose was sideways, in place of her mouth, and where her eyes should have been were a pair of seamlessly stitched ears. Henk stepped away from the silent woman, only then noticing that her arms and legs had been switched. "Somehow, I don't think she was born like that," he said.

"What are you saying? The Puppeteer and the Potato Head are working together?"

Henk didn't *want* to say it, but there was no other explanation. "We've never seen two of them working together before."

There was a jelly-like movement from the doorway behind them. "Au contraire, mon Perrier."

Henk raised his sword to the threat while Dave positioned his shield, ready to defend either of them.

The Potato Head was an ever-changing jumble of human and animal body parts. Right now, it had chosen to be composed of human ears. If it were to touch either one of them, they'd end up looking like the woman on the floor. The Potato Head morphed, every inch of its body covered in baboon lips. "Something big is coming, boys," the lips slurred in unison.

197

"Something far bigger than the three of us. Now, *I'd* wanted to keep you guys alive long enough to see it for yourselves, but the Puppeteer has a knack for making people do things his way . . ."

Dave charged the amorphous shape, slamming the car panel into its malleable flesh and driving it into the opposite wall. Henk was close behind with the sharpened bumper, hacking first at the creature's lower half to disable it, then anywhere he could find an opening. The Potato Head's surface shifted once (covered in toenails) then again (puppy tails) before falling still. Before they could catch their breath, however, it began to rise once more, only now it was being controlled by threads that had crept along the ceiling unnoticed.

"Follow them!" Henk shouted, running into the corridor without looking back. To continue fighting with so many threads around would be certain death. They followed the glistening worms through to a waiting room packed with stacking chairs, then down another corridor marked SURGERY. A single swinging door ahead, from which countless threads were trailing, snaking along the walls, ceiling, and each other on their way to find hosts.

"This must be it."

Dave charged the door.

The Puppeteer was a small creature, roughly Dave's height, whittled out of aged pine by some demonic force in one dimension or another. To compensate for his small stature and brittle body, he'd been given the threads, which took him from one of the least-threatening entities to ever stalk the streets of Sorrow to one of the most dangerous. His splintered face bore the same surprised look as always (as he could not change it), with thick, black eyebrows taking up most of the thin forehead above his wide, painted eyes. He had a black pencil moustache and a red and blue suit, which had always reminded Henk of a nutcracker. "We meet again," he said, his lower lip-smacking against his upper with each wooden word. "Only this time, I have friends." He raised both thin arms to the ceiling. Several blue curtains along the room were thrown open to reveal a handful of men and women in blue surgical gowns. They hopped from their beds to the floor as one, walking awkwardly as though being controlled. Which they were.

The man closest to Henk moaned through a closed mouth, fully aware of what was happening but unable to do anything about it. Henk didn't want to kill the man, but if it came to it . . .

The Puppeteer cackled, his laugher like kindling popping in an open fire as he flexed his fingers, advancing his platoon. A red-haired woman neared Dave, arms outstretched, tears rolling silently down her blushing cheeks. Dave slammed into her with the shield, sent her tumbling into the man behind her, who had been holding a scalpel. Both of them tripped backwards, blood spurting from one of them, or perhaps both—it was impossible to tell.

"Be careful!" Henk said.

"What am I supposed to do?" Dave said defensively. "They're going to kill us if they get the chance."

Henk ducked a fist as the moaning man lashed out. He side-stepped another. Then, cornered between a set of drawers and a hospital bed, Henk drew the serrated bumper along the man's throat and pushed him away. "Fuck it," he said. "KILL THEM ALL!"

The Puppeteer made a noise that could have been surprise as the two men cut/beat their way through the innocents to reach him, aware there was more at stake than the lives of a few randoms and willing to do anything to put a stop to Maria's dastardly plan.

"You couldn't just let us pass, could you?" Dave said, reaching the Puppeteer first. He moved to smash the wooden man about the head but was halted before he could follow through, lifted into the air by a multitude of glistening threads.

"No!" Henk screamed, too busy fending off the threads that were going for him to free his brother. They began to take control.

Dave was lowered to the ground, his face stoic. He slapped the front of his car panel shield with an open hand then began to walk towards Henk.

"Fight it!" Henk spun three-sixty, severing several threads that had been coming at him from all directions.

Dave closed the gap and bashed Henk in the side.

"Stop!" Henk attempted to dodge a second strike but was distracted by the unending waves of snaking thread shooting towards him and took the full force of Dave's shield to his chest, knocking the wind from him. A third strike sent the bumper-sword skidding across the vinyl flooring. It was promptly lifted into the air by yet another bunch of threads and carried away. Henk wheezed. "Dave, please."

Then, he was treading air. A stinging sensation burned at the back of his wrists, elbows, knees, the base of his skull, his ankles.

He was paralysed.

The Puppeteer cackled once again. "Much better. Whatever are we going to do with you troublemakers?"

Henk tried to fight his body as it straightened and stepped into the middle of the aisle, facing Dave. He was able to move his eyes but little else. Dave's body was now facing him, their noses almost touching, staring helplessly into one another's eyes. The skinny leg on Henk's head dangled uselessly between them, and he could feel his brother's finger-brows tickling his forehead.

Searing pain exploded in Henk's groin as Dave's knee connected with it. He then felt his own knee lifting, returning the favour, watched as Dave's eyes grew watery. He could hear the Puppeteer clapping gleefully to his right as they stepped apart and raised their fists to each other. The bastard was going to make them fight to the death.

Then, a deafening roar.

An explosion tossed him into a dreamless night.

Henk coughed up a wad of thick phlegm as he rolled himself onto his stomach. Someone was screaming nearby, but he was unable to pinpoint it. Keeping his eyes open was taking every bit of concentration he had. Another muted explosion showered him with dust and small pieces of rubble. Henk lifted his head, expecting to see the Puppeteer, but instead found a large hole in the wall where the wooden bastard had been standing.

Faint footsteps echoed, approaching. "You're okay. We need to keep moving. It's not safe."

He was lifted to his feet. The room swayed in front of him momentarily, then Dave stepped into his line of sight and slapped him hard across the face. "Thanks, man," Henk said, rubbing his cheek. "I needed that."

"Thank me later. The Baby is headed this way."

The Baby was one entity the Sons of Sorrow hadn't been able to take care of themselves, having to instead rely on the military to gun it down. The Baby's cries were enough to shatter glass and rupture eardrums, and as if that wasn't bad enough, it had an unhealthy obsession with explosives and was able to make one from almost anything.

They charged through the hole in the wall, and sure enough, at the end of the street, a little purple figure was crawling along the middle of the road, a blue bonnet on its head and (thankfully) a yellow dummy in its mouth, which it sucked with gusto as it knocked a grenade together out of objects found in the pockets of the surrounding corpses.

They pressed themselves behind a sign boasting *Plastic Surgery Cheaper Than a Pack of Smokes!* and watched as the

Baby hurled the grenade through the doorway of a nearby shop. There was a high-pitch scream, followed by an explosion of broken glass and blood.

The Baby was too cool to stick around to watch. Instead, it was already crafting the next bomb.

Henk and Dave ran in the opposite direction, taking the longer but (hopefully) safer route to the forest, ignoring the skinned corpses that hung from the lamp posts along the road, and the cat-that-most-certainly-would-not-be-a-cat if they were to look at it directly.

"TAKE MY CHILD!" someone screamed.

"NO, NOT ME! LOOK HOW TASTY MY KID LOOKS!" cried another.

The sounds of death and desperation seeped from every building they passed. There was no way they could help them all, so they opted to help none, reasoning that the faster they could make it to the woods to close the Rift, the sooner they could stop more entities from coming through.

Or so they hoped.

Chapter 20

"MARIA!" Henk yelled as they stepped into the trees. Shimmering blue light filtered through the gaps in the ancient sentinels and cast an almost glittery hue to the air. "YOU HERE?"

Dave cupped his hands to his mouth. "MARIAAAA."

Their calls garnered no response, not that it mattered—they would be heading toward the dazzling light regardless. They trudged across the forest floor for what felt like an eternity. Eventually, they reached the source of the illumination. Looking around, it became apparent they'd been led to the exact place they'd discovered the original Rift all those years ago—just ten minutes outside of town.

As expected, the Rift had grown exponentially since the last time they'd seen it. The thin, membranous layer was still present across its surface, but the inner section now pulsed almost erotically, a cool blue that was brighter in some patches than in others. There was sporadic movement inside.

"Holy anomaly," Henk said, flinching as a bat-winged figure the size of a man emerged from the skin and over the trees.

"How the heck are we going to deal with *that*?" Dave asked.

"You're not."

"Maria!"

"Henk . . . Dave," Maria sneered. She stepped out from behind the mammoth egg, kicking her fiancé's head in front of her like a football. "Good of you to finally piece it together. Tell me, what was it that gave it away? Finding his body?" She kicked the pale head once more. "Or that idiot, the Knob Goblin?"

Henk held a hand to the space between them, showing they were not looking for a fight. She'd been watching their movements all along, waiting to see what they would do when they found Harman. If only Henk had listened to his brother and allowed Harman's body to be dealt with properly . . . "Maria, we need to destroy that thing and close the Rift before it's too late. People are being slaughtered all over town."

"GOOD!" Maria screeched. She ran her fingertips along the glowing blue egg-shaped horror as if in awe of it. "It's already too late. A betrothed's blood has been spilt over the Rift."

"Come home with us," Dave offered, unwilling to humour her ravings. "We'll have a takeaway, smoke a little mo-gro, maybe—"

"I DON'T WANT ANY FUCKING MO-GRO" she screamed.

Henk shot daggers at Dave, urging him not to say anything that may worsen the situation.

Maria continued, shoulders slumped: "Do you still not get it? Do you think it would be possible for *anyone* to be happy with the life I've had?"

Henk shook his head slowly, reluctant to speak. He'd always admired her for her positivity and her kindness. Had it all been an act?

"Of course it's fucking not! That's all it ever was with you two. *'Ohh, let's drink, let's get high, let's go kill something'*. And then, when I'm practically throwing myself to you, all wrapped

205

up in a little bow," she stared at Henk, the blue light casting eerie shadows across her face, "you up and leave without so much as a proper goodbye? You should have *known* I was just as stressed here as the pair of you. Only I *couldn't* leave because I'd be leaving my *asshole* stepdad alone with my mum. At least with me around, he wouldn't take it out on her. But you guys were too busy getting wasted all the time to even notice, weren't you?"

"Wait," Henk said. Had he really been that oblivious? Sure, their lives back then had been a bit of a drunken, drug-fuelled, dead-parents haze, but surely he would have noticed if the girl he was obsessed with was being abused . . . wouldn't he?

"All I wanted was for you to help me," Maria moaned. "You should have seen. Even Harman saw. But no. You up and leave me to deal with my shitty life in this shitty town without so much as an apology."

"I'm so sorry," Henk began. He took a step toward her, trying to maintain a calm front while terrified of whatever it was that was starting to claw at the inside of the egg. "I honestly had no idea things were so bad. You always seemed so happy."

"Typical fucking man," Maria spat. She produced a multitool from her jacket pocket and flicked the blade out. "It's too late for sorry. We're all going to die together."

"NO!" Dave screamed. He ran at Maria, but it was too late; her blade had already torn a sizeable hole in the side of the egg and agitated the monster within.

There was the sound of ripping plastic as the tear widened, and a flood of gunky black fluid rushed out, sweeping Maria off her feet and casting her away. The membranous shell stretched in all directions as the large object writhed. Flashes of sickly-peach flesh peeked from the tear. The egg ruptured, and the creature exploded into the world.

Henk ducked for cover behind the nearest tree while Dave leapt into a shallow ditch, unable to resist sneaking a glimpse of the monstrosity as it unfolded itself and shed its blue wrapping. Henk screamed Maria's name but could hardly hear himself over the creaking of the creature's limbs as it rose above them, blotting out the sunlight with its broad shoulders.

"What the hell is that?!" Dave shouted.

Henk had to crane his neck to see the top of the creature.

The massive shape stood like a man on two legs, had two arms, two shoulders, but no head. Tall as at least fifty stacked Stephen Hawkings, the smooth, peachy figure was hairless, genderless. It stretched its lanky arms high above its head and rotated its wrists. Then, as its arms came back down, several glowing blue snakes protruded from its neck-hole, sniffing at the air as if searching for something. Several stood erect, pointing dead ahead, and it was then that Henk saw they were capped with nails, the same as the fingers that had been terrorising the town. The rest of the fingers followed suit, tasting the air. Henk threw himself out of the path of the truck-sized feet that razed a trail through the forest in the direction the fingers were pointing.

Chapter 21

Henk and Dave were falling behind. Fortunately, it was easy to keep an eye on the route of the headless giant as it walked sluggishly through the centre of town—if they were to lose sight of it somehow, they could simply follow the trail of destruction.

Sorrow had seen better days. Fires were rife throughout the main strip, and they were able to walk straight through where the library had stood just moments before until it was flattened by a gargantuan foot. Smushed into the footprints here and there were bloodied splatters, squashed flat against brick dust and compacted books. Even the other entities were keeping a safe distance from the behemoth as it kicked its way through buildings, parks and children. Henk knew precisely what it was going for.

The Head.

It had always been about the Head. How had he not seen it before? Sure, it did not appear to be a threat on its own, but since it had been feeding, growing, it had been able to regurgitate its meals through the fingers into the egg, feeding its body. The energy produced by this process must be enough to bring others to their world.

Harman's blood, the blood of a betrothed, had been all it needed to finish the process and break free. Maria must have been planning this for quite some time. It was unlikely to come together accidentally with all the variables at play.

Maria.

They hadn't been able to find her after she was washed away by the vile amniotic fluid, which meant she had either drowned or escaped. Dave had managed to pull Henk away from the scene, slapping him across the face repeatedly to remind him of the slightly more pressing issue at hand. What they would do if they ever caught up to it was a matter they'd have to deal with when it came to it.

Henk dodged a poison dart fired from the Reek's blowgun (yet another entity back from the dead), casting only a cursory glance at the radioactive man as six children jumped him. Their parents slipped by unnoticed.

"Where is it taking us?" Dave panted. Neither of them were particularly fit, but Dave's love of all things smokeable was coming back to bite him.

"Not sure," Henk responded between breaths. Knowing they couldn't keep running for much longer, he suggested they slow their pace. It was leading them out to the Notabaddie farm. And if it continued further?

Well, then it would be someone else's problem.

The headless giant slowed as it reached the outskirts of the farmland.

"What's it doing?" Dave whispered as if the thing without a head would hear him.

The Shades were gathered by the front gates, having been conditioned to protect the owner's land at all costs. The giant swatted them with an open hand and sent them reeling through the skies like a swarm of bluebottles, despite their inability to be touched by any means mortal. The monster's neck-fingers danced excitedly before stiffening in the direction of a large green barn, leading it onwards. Henk reached the main gates and decided he was happy to hang back a moment.

The giant slid both hands beneath the lip of the barn's roof and tore it clean off with the ease of flipping a table. Henk gestured for Dave to stay hidden as it lifted something from within.

The Head's eyes rolled frantically as the hands lifted it over the neck stump, the fingers from either part reaching for one another. They intertwined, then pulled themselves together seamlessly. It gasped, wobbled as if drunk, then collapsed into the barn in a hail of splintered wood and twisted metal but was back on its feet instantly.

"What's it doing?" Dave asked, struggling to see from his position.

"Finding its feet."

The creature pushed itself upright and rolled its shoulders like a weightlifter warming up. It groaned as its fingers lengthened until they collided with the floor at its feet.

"There's no way we can take that thing on."

The fingers started to rise from the ground, pulsing ocean blue as they snaked off in seemingly random directions. Some poked through doors and smashed through windows of nearby storage shacks and stables, snatching anything hiding within. A donkey and a Shade were first to emerge, the fingers suctioning the prey and lifting them to the Head's mouth. The creature grimaced as it spat out the Shade. It swallowed the donkey whole. One of the elongated fingers broke away from the rest of the pack and began to slither across the floor toward the gates.

"Now," Henk said.

They moved in opposite directions, keeping low as they moved along the cobbled wall in either direction until they each felt it was safe to hop over and run for the nearest cover. The Head's fingers appeared to sense them, acting independently of the creature they were attached to as they adjusted their pathing to face the humans. Henk ducked behind an overturned wheelbarrow and waited until a finger skirted over his location. He then sprinted to a tractor, pressed his back against it. Dave was keeping level with him, crawling through a small field of cabbages. There was a horrifying bleeting as the giant's fingers sniffed out a pen of goats, snatching them up and lowering them down to the giant's mouth like a foreign delicacy. Henk used the momentary distraction to round the tractor and advanced to a piece of rusted machinery that turned out to be much smaller than he'd thought. The fingers were already sniffing out fresh prey, and there was nothing between his position and the house that could provide suitable cover.

"OVER HERE!" Henk snapped his head in Dave's direction. The fool was standing upright, smacking two cabbages together to attract the giant's attention.

He was going to get himself killed.

Then again, given the number of fingers flicking through the air, there wasn't anything he could do that would end up with them *not* being killed.

Henk broke into a sprint, skirting junk as he made a beeline for the front door of the dilapidated Notabaddie residence. He heard Dave utter a startled cry behind him but didn't dare to look back. He was so close.

The fresh air that rushed in the front door with him was not enough to mask the stench of rot. The interior was somehow even more deteriorated than it had been the day before; large sections of the floorboards had rotten and fallen through, offering a nausea-inducing view down to the collapsed basement. At least with the monster standing outside, the chances of its fingers rising from the depths were far less.

Then again, who really knew how it worked?

The telephone was an old rotary dial, yellowed with age and half-hidden beneath a stack of damp paperbacks. Henk was equally relieved as he was surprised to hear it still had a dial tone. He stuck his index finger in the dial wheel. The plastic was stuck. "Shit!" He applied more pressure, hoping it was just stiff from age, but the brittle finger wheel snapped off and skittered across the room.

Without backup, there was no hope.

A blinding flash of blue light whipped through the broken window in the front room and buried itself in the wall next to his head. Henk ran for the back door and out into the open field beyond as seven additional fingers erupted through the house's roof and walls, made a fist, then brought the entire structure down in a cloud of dust. Henk was struck in the calf by a chunk of spinning brick and collapsed to his knees.

This was it.

It was funny, really; he'd spent half his life wishing he were dead, yet now he was staring it in the face he wanted to live more than ever. Or was it simply his instincts kicking in? The overriding desire to survive no matter what.

The giant's fingers stopped just short of him. Ten fat, throbbing digits wavering in the air, inches from his face. The ground shook as the giant's shins crashed through the ruins of the Notabaddie estate, catching up to them. The giant's fingers retracted, returned to their 'regular' size.

Was it playing with him?

"Henk!"

"Dave?!" Henk sat up. He was sure he'd heard his brother's voice but could not see him anywhere.

"Up here!"

Henk couldn't believe it. Dave was perched on the giant's shoulder, waving with both arms. "I thought you were dead! What are you doing up there?!"

"I think it's my face-fingers . . . it doesn't want to hurt me."

Henk looked down to the tangle of fingers that had replaced the hair on his arms, all that was left from his high earlier in the day. The giant's eyes were no longer spinning. Small, electric blue pupils appeared to be showing some kind of recognition. "It must be the mo-gro," he shouted. "It doesn't see us as a threat. "Get down, it's too dangerous!"

"Fuck that. You come up here! This is awesome!"

The giant lowered itself to its knees and placed a hand flat on the floor as if it understood. Henk mounted the nearest mountainous knuckle, keeping a safe distance from the crackling fingers, and allowed himself to be lifted to the giant's opposite shoulder despite his better judgment. He wrapped his arms around its neck as it stood upright, thankful he did not suffer from vertigo.

His elevated position offered a view of the entire town and beyond. Black smoke choked the skyline, polluting what would typically have been a postcard sunset. St Augustine's had been levelled at some point. Small figures were parading a large wooden cross through the streets, with what looked to be an obese man nailed to it. A sizeable electrical shockwave erupted in the town square, and several people could be heard crying for help as blasts of lightning struck the buildings around it. Everywhere he looked, was death and destruction.

The giant stood still as if awaiting instruction, its sinewy shoulders rising and falling with each heavy breath. Finally, Henk said, "We can't just sit here and watch everyone die."

"What else are we going to do? It's not like we can do anything to save them."

"SAVE," the giant growled, its voice reverberating like a gunshot in a tunnel.

"Y-you talk now?" Dave asked.

"Do you understand us?" Henk added.

The giant exhaled heavily through its mouth by way of response.

Henk tried again: "Save town. Protect Sorrow."

"PROTECT."

"Yo, hang on a minute." Dave scampered on top of the giant's head, flat on his belly to peer down at Henk. "If the only reason it's not murdering us is because of the mo-gro, we can't take it anywhere near town. It'll kill everything it sees."

"But if we don't do something soon, everyone's going to be dead anyway."

"Huh." Dave propped his chin in his hands and kicked his legs up behind him. Henk wished he could adapt to the ever-maddening situation with the same level of indifference. "So, what are we suggesting?"

Henk grit his teeth. "Do you think you can steer this thing?"

"STEER," the Head said.

Dave stood, taking a wide stance to balance on top of the flat head. He thrust a finger forward. "ONWARD!"

The Head lurched, took a wide stride in the direction Dave was pointing. "Where to?" he yelled to Henk.

"Back to the Rift. Stick to the fields and avoid the town."

215

Chapter 22

The giant was surprisingly compliant.

Henk and Dave shared a joint of mo-gro on the journey to ensure the beast would stay friendly, and now had wriggling fingers protruding from their cheeks, lips, and chins. A few times along the way, they'd had to scold the Head as it sent its bioluminescent fingers off in the direction of town, but for the most part, it was very good at listening to them.

"Where's it gone?" Dave shouted over the thundering footsteps.

The membranous shell had already deteriorated, although the black gunk that had erupted from it still caked the surrounding areas. "Holy . . ." The sunken pit left behind was overflowing with mo-gro, enough of the glowing bud to fill several skips.

"Heck," Dave muttered. "What now?"

"Isn't it obvious? If the only reason it's not attacking us is because of the fingers, then we need to make sure the rest of the people still alive out there have them too." Saying it out loud sounded ridiculous, but this was his life now.

"Right on," Dave said, then proceeded to instruct the giant to gather handfuls of the mo-gro' and hurl it in the direction of the fires raging about town. An hour or so later, a sweet-tasting neon-blue fog had settled across the land for miles in every direction.

SIX MONTHS LATER

After the town was cleared of any entities unwilling to play ball, the long rebuilding process began. Sorrow was put back together over the following months with the help of the giant—under Dave's supervision—and a lot of additional funding from third parties with interest in capitalising off the tragedy. The fact that you had to smoke a bowl of mo-gro before entering the town's borders was enough to put some visitors off, but to others, it simply made the experience even more memorable. There were plenty of children running about with fingers covering their faces (upon the parent's insistence that the volunteers working the ticket booths bend the new rules and allow children—in case of emergencies).

Sorrow was prospering like never before. The new council had elected to erect a monument for those who had died during the attack, and a second, in the town square, to act as a deterrent to anyone looking to bring future harm to the town. Henk had been unsure about it at first but eventually came around to the idea of casting Maria in concrete. The statue had several intricate breathing holes as well as a feeding funnel and waste drainage, ensuring she would be kept alive with nothing to do but think about what she'd done.

"Good boy. Play nice. I'll be back for you this afternoon," Dave said, patting Stumpy on the head.

"ME NICE," Stumpy responded. The giant had never shown any objection to Dave's pet name for it, so it had stuck. Dave slid down Stumpy's arm, then watched him walk away with the pride of a farmer watching his son fuck a prize pig. "They sure grow up fast, don't they?"

Henk rolled his eyes. He still thought it was a little weird that Dave and the giant had become so close, but never let it bother him—their relationship was far from the strangest thing in town, what with every man, woman and child walking around with a body covered in fingers. Across the town square, the Head perched on the purpose-built bench, where it would spend the rest of the morning posing for selfies with visitors and signing billboard-sized posters.

The brothers approached a large neoclassical building constructed on the grounds of the recently demolished Two Trees College. A sizeable crowd had gathered on the front lawn, waiting behind a length of red ribbon for the guests of honour to arrive.

"Ah, and here they are now. Please, make way for the heroes of this story: the Wolfe Brothers!"

They waved away the screams and applause as they made their way through the middle of the crowd, smiling and nodding politely at the requests to sign breasts, penises, and baby's eyelids. "Thank you, Brett," Henk said, taking his place on the front ramp of the Benderson Museum of Sorrow Memorabilia, next to the suited man in the wheelchair. "Wouldn't miss this for the world."

Dave took the novelty-sized pair of scissors from the Shade to Brett's right. "If you knew Brett as we do, you'd know this has been a dream for much of his life. It's great to see him taking his—at times—unhealthy obsession," he winked at Brett, "and put it to use in a way that benefits not only the town but also each and every one of us."

Colour rose to Brett's cheeks, unsure of where Dave's unscripted speech would go next. During his near-death experience in the mayor's mansion, he'd promised whatever was in charge of the afterlife he would come clean about the identity of the Knob Goblin if he were to survive, and he *would* . . . at some point. Just not right now, not like this, in front of so many people, at the grand opening of his life's work.

Fortunately, Dave's speech changed tracks: "Without Brett's help during the investigation, none of us would be standing here today, and for that, we will forever be in his debt."

Henk pulled the ribbon taut in both hands and presented it to Dave. "It is with great honour that we declare this museum—"

"Open," Dave said, snipping the ribbon in two with a comical *clack!*

The crowd whooped as they surged up the wide ramp and into the building, each person present desperate to be the first in history to snap a picture of the exhibits and upload them to the 'gram. Once the initial rush had tapered off, the others followed at their own pace, with Brett taking the lead in his electric wheelchair, weaving as they entered the bustling entrance, the sound of fingers clicking and rubbing against one another echoing around the cavernous room. They stared up at the plasticised and suspended corpses of the Gloved King and his troupe of backup dancers as the queue slowly filtered past the ticket booths. "It's more than I could ever have dreamed of. If you hadn't come back to check on me . . ."

Henk chuckled. "You've thanked us quite enough. Without your help, the entire town would have been gone before we even knew what was going on."

"Perhaps," he said as the Pale Groper waved them through the ticketing area and into the lobby proper, "but my crime-fighting days are over. The attack on the town was just the thing I needed to get this place up and running."

"Word," Dave said, distracted by a tall glass case containing Pinkypaw's severed head.

They moved in content silence as they toured the many exhibits of the sprawling museum, stopping now and then to recall tales of how they'd foiled Maria's dastardly plans and cleared up the town with the help of the Head to anyone that would listen. Eventually, they reached the gift shop, and the space guests could pose for commemorative photographs, smiling as a mother sacrificed her young daughter to a life-sized casting of the Yellow Hammer. At the same time, the photographer instructed her to scream louder.

Seeing the joy all the death could bring to the masses was one of the many reasons Henk had decided to stay and try and make another go of life in Sorrow. His fame meant there was no shortage of women offering their numbers, requests for TV and movie cameos, and countless paid interviews. They had their own a chat show in the works, on which survivors of bizarre attacks could come and talk about their experiences. There were even plans for a segment at the end where the entity responsible would be brought out to apologise in front of the live audience (if it were still alive).

For the first time, things were looking up. Sure, it might not be the future he'd envisioned for himself, but life could be funny like that; even the people you've put on a pedestal can let you down. Henk shoved his hands in his pockets as he left the museum and descended the stone stairs. He passed Dave (rubbing his finger-filled face against the finger-filled face of a blonde woman) on his way through the throng of tourists wandering the gardens. He came to a stop in front of Concrete Maria, kissed his finger, then touched it to her shin.

He'd never know at which point in her life she had cracked, but now they would always have each other.

Whether she knew it or not.

THE END

Afterword

When I set out to write this book, I had the intention of writing a collection of short stories based in and around a sinister village. The idea would have seen me write each story from a different character's point of view, while the plot eventually evolved, and things would start to make a little more sense when retold from another perspective. The idea would have seen the book ending with a big reveal; that most of the villagers were being controlled by a demonic entity living beneath the church. The entity would achieve this by reaching through the ground under the village with thin, finger-like stems that ran from its own body to the back of villager's heads.

I planned on using Henk and Dave as the 'main' characters, with each story centred around the bizarre people they interacted with, but I ended up liking them too much not to focus on them the entire time, and somehow ended up ditching the short story collection idea without even realising I'd done it until about halfway in.

If you made it to the end, I'd like to thank you for reading. And for sticking around to read this. And this. And this.

Thank you to my wonderful beta readers, Marcie Robinson, Melissa Potter, Augustus Roe, and Corrina Morse. And a huge thank you to Madeleine Swan, Luke Kondor, Reekfeel, and Heather Moffitt. You're the best!

About the Author

Matthew A. Clarke writes horror, bizarro, and anything in between.

He has authored four novels and two novellas, where he explores themes of loyalty, acceptance, and betrayal. He has also had many short stories published, ranging from humorous to the horrific. His shorter pieces, usually from his darker side, can be found in several Black Hare Press anthologies, KJK Publishing, Hellbound Books, and many more.

Bibliography

Coffin Dodgers, Self-Published, 2021
Things Were Easier Before You Became a Giant Fucking Mantis, Self-Published, 2021
Beyond Human, Black Hare Press, 2021
Those That Remain, Black Hare Press, 2021
The World Has Gone to Turd and the Only Way to Save It Is With a Big 'Ol Battle Royale, Planet Bizarro, 2021
Sons of Sorrow, Planet Bizarro, 2022

Connect

Facebook: www.facebook.com/matthewaclarkeauthor

CPSIA information can be obtained
at www.ICGtesting.com
Printed in the USA
LVHW021534240322
714284LV00002B/111